Empathy
Beyond
Imagination

Ten Short Stories

Bryan C. Hazelton, LCSW CASAC BCD

abbott press

Abbott Press books may be ordered through booksellers or by contacting:

Abbott Press
1663 Liberty Drive
Bloomington, IN 47403
www.abbottpress.com
Phone: 1 (866) 697-5310

Because of the dynamic nature of the Internet, any web addresses or
links contained in this book may have changed since publication and
may no longer be valid. The views expressed in this work are solely those
of the author and do not necessarily reflect the views of the publisher,
and the publisher hereby disclaims any responsibility for them.

Interior Image Credit: Bryan C. Hazelton

ISBN: 978-1-4582-2055-4 (sc)
ISBN: 978-1-4582-2054-7 (hc)
ISBN: 978-1-4582-2053-0 (e)

Library of Congress Control Number: 2016917760

Print information available on the last page.

Abbott Press Revised Edition date: 12/21/2019

DEDICATION

I dedicate this book to my brave great grandparents some 11 generations past. John Howland and his wife to be Elizabeth Tilley, along with her parents, Mr. and Mrs. John and Joan (Hurst) Tilley, were passengers on the Mayflower in 1620.

During a turbulent storm John Howland was swept into the sea. Grabbing hold of a "topsail halyard," (a rope) he was rescued from the stormy Atlantic. Although Elizabeth's parents sadly did not survive the winter, both Elizabeth and John did, and were later married...

FOREWORD

True stories fill the hearts and minds of psychotherapists. Fictional stories, written by this therapist, fill the pages of this book.

At the heart of Psychotherapy is empathy, emotionally understanding another's experience by imagining their world.

Yes, at times, therapists may steer away from thoughts or feelings, expressed or triggered by a patient and fail to be empathic. Although we must accept these shortcomings, we cannot be complacent monitoring them. The range of impact from "empathic failures" can vary from microscopic and common, to severe and tragic. At times, they can contribute to grave outcomes, such as suicide or murder. Sometimes it's challenging for a therapist to empathically sense furious rage or unrelenting despair. Being emotionally tuned in is critical, as we may be the last line of defense in preventing tragedies.

Some readers may feel that passages or themes of this book are disturbing, provocative or inappropriate. Yet, if we can't allow ourselves to imagine unusual or disturbing content in *fictional stories*, how can we imagine alarming intent in patients sitting in front of us?

These unconventional stories counter deeply rooted expectations of what is fair, normal, right or appropriate. They bring us a wider range of our patients' realm by suspending assumptions and opening possibilities. Underlying these stories are layers of American culture woven unexpectedly into these mind-twisting tales. These psychological adventures are novel, entertaining and for all readers!

Please Note: These stories do not intend to characterize patients or psychotherapists in a negative light. Nor does the book intend to suggest any particular professional or personal guidance.

Bryan C. Hazelton LCSW, CASAC, BCD

CONTENTS

2047

Imagine it is the year 2047. Joseph and his family are celebrating the 3rd birthday of his grandson, Conrad. Happiness and harmony rule the event.

Now imagine being back in 2019 and you are Joseph's Psychotherapist. He is attending treatment solely due to pressure from his family, who along with Joseph, have been negatively affected by his alcoholism. He sees no problem and is completely unaware that his life is on the line.

You're doing your best to keep him in therapy so he'll recognize the seriousness of his problem. A tall order indeed.

You face the crucial responsibility of working with Joseph in the isolation of your office. Just you and he, except not in any usual sense. Imagine there's no walls or ceiling to your office. Invisible to mere mortals is an apparition-like, circular row of seating that surrounds you and Joseph. Each seat is next to and slightly higher than the last. They spiral upwards, broadening as they reach endlessly into the sky. Seated and looking down with piqued interest are Joseph's prospective descendants. Neither you nor Joseph can see or hear them, yet they are captivated by every spoken word. They loudly applaud your confronting statements, while they agonize over Joseph's denial.

Tens of thousands of onlookers, fully aware that if Joseph is unsuccessful **at** attaining recovery, he'll soon die in a horrific drinking and driving accident. If that were to occur, his descendants would fail to be born, as Joseph had not yet had children.

Imagine a multitude of souls, rooting and cheering for the success of Joseph's therapy. One can only imagine their intense engagement, as *his* success means life for *them*!

Although you may be a Psychotherapist to one solitary person, the benefits can expand exponentially to others.

How many moments loved by so many are created? A moment is born in 2047, as a beaming Conrad peddles his birthday tricycle on the colorful slates of Grandpa Joe's patio.

The End

Bound
and
Constrained

CHAPTER 1

It started as innocent curiosity. Roland's Patient cancelled again, this time due to "being out of town." Since Roland's commute home crossed within two rights and a left of his Patient's house, he thought it'd be harmless to ride by and see for himself. Although Roland couldn't confirm his Patient was telling the truth, a positive ID would verify that he wasn't. "What could possibly be wrong with that?" he thought. "No one will know and it'll help me understand my Patient!"

Roland felt lightheaded as he approached his Patient's house. His heart was pounding as he caught sight of Hank on the porch. "There he is! And he's drinking! I knew it! I knew he was lying to me! This only proves that activity outside the office helps the therapy! My supervisor Ned," he said exaggeratedly looking to the sky, "and his lectures on neutrality and containment. I feel so bound, so constrained by him!"

Moving forward with his practice of Psychotherapy, Roland's "success" with Hank justified further activity "to help" his Patients. Although careful not to be seen, he didn't think of consequences. Roland was neither troubled, nor conflicted and in fact, felt quite alive when acting out-side.

Months later, Roland's new Patient Florence, shared that she was harassed while driving on the highway. As Roland began to compassionately imagine being a victim of road rage, his Patient revealed, "They beep at me over and over, it's so rude! So I keep my distance by driving all the way over to the left. Yet then they beep louder!"

Suddenly Roland's sympathetic leaning tipped, spilling into rage. "What the hell!" he said to himself. "That's the passing lane! I hate when people block the fast lane!" His feelings brimmed to the outer edge of control, but controlled they were.

Roland was scheduled to see his supervisor Ned on Tuesday. He hoped to present Florence's session in a measured manner, as supervision made him nervous. Roland hated being subject to his "all-knowing" overseer. He was *certain* from their first meeting that Ned just wanted him to feel small and weak-minded.

Walking into Ned's office, Roland was startled by his own anxiety and lost all words. His careful reserve evaporated, leaving him in a state of jumbled confusion and red-raw frustration.

Ned had his scalpel ready, surgically probing with incisive questions, cutting to the heart of the matter.

"I read your progress notes and understand you felt strongly about your Patient's report of driving. Did you show in words or body language your personal feelings? Have you identified **the** source of your counter-transference? Did you sense your Patient was aware of how you felt? What are you feeling now as you relate this to me?"

Quickly pulling himself together, he conveyed what transpired with Florence. Roland dodged the point of Ned's questions, focusing instead on Florence's passive-aggressive driving.

Ned encouraged Roland to remain neutral with Florence, as it was too early in her treatment to risk a narcissistic injury.

Roland resisted, attempting to drive home the point riding circles in his mind. "How is she ever going to learn, if she is not taught?"

But no, his supervisor would not entertain that question. Instead he reiterated the usual party line. "Over time the process of therapy will help her choose more adaptive behaviors."

As the door closed behind him, Roland barely noticed fellow clinicians passing in the hall. His mind was racing, "This is bull! If I'm ever gonna help someone, I have to do it *my way*! Florence just needs a 'corrective experience.' It's simple, in fact, I know what will help her!"

In a mere 45 minutes he had devised an elaborate scheme. It would be obvious to an observer—had there been one—that his plan far exceeded any wish to help. Furthermore, it wasn't visible by self-examination, as there was no mirror directed within.

On the day of his Patient's next appointment, the rental car and disguise were all set. When Florence left the office to drive the 6 miles home, Roland slipped out the back, swiftly seeking his vehicle of deception. Eyes darting, he located the two cars and entered his, fumbling with the key out of fear he would lose her. Florence drove away as his key found the ignition. He was flushed with an adrenalin rush, so much so, that he forgot the touch of wearing a beard and wig disguise. He finished applying it when he spied her in the fast lane several cars ahead. Within minutes he maneuvered his vehicle to mercilessly tailgate her, alternating between aggressively driving in front of and along side her. It was as if he was getting even with every driver who had ever wronged him.

Finally out of concern for her life, she moved to another lane. Roland excitedly sped past her, with a smile he couldn't contain. "Success! That's what she needed! It's so satisfying to help people! Outside activity does work!" Turning back, he realized he was late for his next Patient. "That damn supervisor! Always peering through the cracks! If I hadn't had to be so careful, I'd be on time!"

CHAPTER 2

An unbiased look at Roland's training revealed no paucity of professional guidance or education through his 2 years of direct practice. A full spectrum of ethical issues had been delineated by various institutions, a licensing board, and by Ned himself. The value of non-judgmental neutrality, along with the complications of dual relationships, was strongly emphasized.

Ned toiled with vigor as he attempted to mold Roland into a competent and caring agent of change. But Roland's compelling wish to heal Patients took unexpected turns, which both intrigued and alarmed Ned. His efforts to understand Roland more deeply were stymied by Roland's reappearing mantra, "How are they ever going to learn, if they are not taught?"

Roland did not act out in supervision, well, not exactly. Although he continued to report his clinical work, a growing mass of unreported feelings, thoughts and behaviors grew like a cancer within. Each step of activity furthered his toxic perspective. Like most obsessive symptoms, his multiplied over time, marked by a failure to reflect upon them. What ruled his mind was a rigidified edict of "Right!" and "Wrong!"

At times, Ned recognized Roland's singular focus and wondered about deeper determinants of his thinking. Ned knew he was not naïve to the ways of the world. Roland had achieved honors in post-graduate education and in a previous career had successfully designed men's shirts. Despite those who would say the transferability of skills, experience and approach for these two careers was as different as chalk and cheese, Ned knew their commonality was seeking an internal image that rang true with authenticity.

Time passed as days flowed, numbering into months. Then, as October approached, a convention of the season resulted in further activity.

Roland had been treating a female patient in her 30's for some months. Over time she revealed a history of being victimized by others, mostly men. This troubled Roland. He fantasized about how to help her.

Then, as a major election approached, she openly shared her political affiliation. Roland was deeply struck by her disclosure. Silently, yet internally loud, his mind bellowed, "She's being fooled! I cannot stand by and watch *that* political party replicate her trauma! It is my duty to protect her!"

A plan flew through his mind attaching itself to a mechanism of act. Cautionary internal reviews were by-passed, leaving Roland blindly committed to action.

That next morning at 4 am he went to her home and removed the political lawn signs she had so faithfully laid out only days before.

"The political signs are a reminder of her co-dependency. They reinforce her issues each and every time she sees them!" A smile crossed his face as he warmly reflected on helping his Patient. For after all, "How is she ever going to learn, if she is not taught!"

CHAPTER 3

Meanwhile, supervision had stalled as Roland became more guarded and distant. Ned intuitively sensed reason for concern and brought it to the Clinical Director. Unfortunately Dr. Michael Rooney was not empathic and conveyed to Ned an underlying, you've done something wrong attitude. Attempts by Ned to address Roland's change of attitude only brought frustration, as Roland had become a master at rationalizing.

However, this particular Tuesday Ned took a softer approach by asking Roland about recent clinical insights. Roland immediately became excited, as his wish for recognition betrayed his defenses. He thought to himself, "Ned is finally seeing the light!" Roland seized the moment and said, "It seems to me there's an opportunity with my Patient, George. I understand he has a Facebook page. Since he's so guarded, and resists revealing himself, I can pose as an old friend and try to be friended..."

Ned lost it! "You're considering tricking your Patient through Facebook? That is tantamount to stalking. That is unethical and inappropriate conduct for a Psychotherapist!"

Roland immediately realized his error and deftly responded, "Did you think I was serious? I would never do that! You're misunderstanding me. You've always taught me to have an open mind. I was simply imagining the existing possibilities. There's nothing wrong with thoughts, it's whether one acts upon them is what matters."

Although Ned knew he couldn't trust Roland's explanation, he was relieved to hear it, as it lifted the burden of dismissal. Ned dreaded the idea of such proceedings, so he shelved his immediate concern and committed himself to follow Roland's work more closely and if need be, take disciplinary action at a later date.

At home that night Roland was deeply shaken. "How could I have trusted him? I'll never, ever, make that mistake again!"

Circular blame raced around his mind. On fire with hurt, anger and regret, he could find no relief. Emotions intensified as he paced his apartment floor. Defenses were circumnavigated as conflicts over aggression, his care for others, and his need to control collided within.

Wounded deeply by Ned ignited the many incendiary rungs of a column extending far into Roland's past. His mind raced at a pace of unforgiving intensity, as he became overwhelmed and confused. Then, to maintain mental cohesion, an overarching psyche took hold. He emerged a short time later feeling absolutely certain, certain about everything. No doubts, no questions, no grey area survived. Going forward he was all in. A very scary situation for anyone, except there was no one to see it.

In Roland's mind the answer was right there. He never saw it so clearly. It was simple. He must follow his own convictions. He must follow what he knows to be right! Out loud to no one he ranted, "How are they ever going to learn, if they are not taught? I could get through to them if Ned didn't put the yoke of neutrality around my neck!

I entered this field to straighten the twisted, and flex the rigid. To right wrongs, not be wrong about what's right! Those in need cry out for relief but no one hears them. God knows their suffering and He knows of my commitment to never stand idly by! I cannot allow their pain! Serious situations require serious action!

I act for the betterment of the people, not through any need of my own. I am the surrogate Citizen of good intentions. And yet, my supervisor will never understand! No one will! The Citizen knows the truth. And the truth will set my Patients free! They'll rise from their sleep, freed from the bondage of their afflictions! Freed by the acts of the Citizen.

This world is disturbed. No one sees what's real, only me! That's why I act, to help. Someday they'll understand and I'll hide no more. I'll stand proud knowing I've made all the difference. Until then, I must keep my actions secret for I'm so far ahead of them all."

Roland momentarily became quiet, before bursting further, "Clinical neutrality will be seen in the clarity of its darkness, a blight on the terrain of treatment. Neutrality a sickness of indifference! A monstrous manifestation of non-care!

We are shackled and bound by systematic dogma, fed by so-called professors, passed on through generations of so-called theoreticians. In reality, they spout complex rationalizations, while those in need wither, all for the sake of containment and neutrality. They act as if it benefits Patients, when in truth it's all about them! Sick psychological lies! Sick!!

Let the Citizen be known! A great man! Courageous in my actions, risking that the world will catch on to my brilliance before they catch on to me! My efforts to help are so constrained, so bound by their doctrine!"

CHAPTER 4

Monday morning Roland went to work as usual. Although he didn't appear to be different, his fiery feelings needed little to kindle a fervent mission.

Last week, he and Ned had disagreed over how to treat his new female Patient, Annalise. She had recently made a decision to engage in topless dancing at a local "Gentlemen's Club." Roland was quite troubled by her decision on several fronts, most notably the danger of harm from that business' clientele.

Ned counseled him to be non-judgmental and to simply follow his Patient's lead. But Roland took that counsel literally and began to shadow Annalise. He surreptitiously watched her comings and goings to make sure she was "safe." This frequent exposure fed the flames of his irrationality. Excessive pacing dominated his time, as any semblance of reasonable judgment faded with the setting sun. Another sleepless night under the still black sky, tore at his ability to make sense. Feelings took hold, driving him forward, propelling him to recklessness.

As morning broke, sense and reason lay discarded by the roadside. In the pinball game of life, the "tilt" sign was flashing madly, except there was no one to see it.

Roland called in sick, resting for the night of the corrective experience. By mid afternoon his plan was fully prepared. Roland knew the *only* answer was to scare his Patient away from her new chosen vocation.

That night he went to her place of business dressed in an elaborate, yet obvious disguise. His thick glasses, peeling mustache and gel plastered hair looked absurdly unreal. He sat near the stage so as to engage with her. Little time passed before Annalise recognized him and his pathetic attempt to fool her. Her initial stunned feelings gave way to anger, as curiosity submerged them both. She gave him no sign of recognition.

Later that night, after several verbal exchanges, she yielded to his ruse, and allowed him to drive her home. During the drive pieces fell into place, as she recalled from therapy his restlessness, his far away looks, and the odd grimaces he displayed when she spoke of issues of intimacy.

As they pulled in front of her home she was cautious, not quite knowing what to expect. As they reached her vestibule he made veiled threats of harm to her.

Street smart, she knew his words were empty attempts to alarm her. They did not. Instead they added insult to injury. Swiftly, like the tide rising in a storm, her anger crested. She reached out to smack him and accidently ripped off part of his disguise. A body blow of shame knocked him to the floor.

Annalise barked, "Get up! How dare you show up at my job and try to trick me! You and your lectures about self-control! You can't even restrain yourself. Do you need me to teach you the hard way? Like a child?"

The power differential clicked off and snapped on, with a resounding metal clang. Existing authority was instantly reversed, reshaping the paradigm's flip.

Her threat to report Roland's inappropriate behavior quickly cemented his allegiance to her authority. The Citizen was no more. *He* had had a corrective experience. Transformed, Roland assumed a supplicant obedience to the higher power that appeared before his eyes. This she used to her full advantage.

For years, Annalise wished for someone with a respectable job and a decent salary to take care of her. But most importantly, she wanted someone she could feel safe with. Someone who would dare not hurt her. Now she had him in the flesh. The control of Roland was solely in her hands. This clear and consistent position shaped and defined his being. No longer in conflict over boundary issues, he felt contained and safe. He now knew his place with Annalise and considering how he had treated her, Roland was *"bound"* to learn his lesson every day.

"After all," she would say, as she tightened the restraints, "how is he ever going to learn, if he is not taught?"

THE END

Both Exist

From his chair, Jude could see the roofs of nearby buildings. Horizontal sunrays met with metal, sending shafts of upward light casting the face of Jude beatific.

"Father," he said forlornly, "I feel lost. There's such a gulf between my reason and my faith. How can I bring them together?"

Father Pratt asked, "What do you feel?"

Jude looked within, stating sadly, "It's an alone feeling... emptiness and loneliness consume me."

"You've spoken about these feelings. How is it to feel them?" "They're difficult to tolerate, Father. Feeling vacant and alone without purpose or direction is painful. Yet other times, I feel connected and engaged."

"Yes," Father Pratt said softly, "I understand. Nonetheless, feelings of disconnection will help pave the way to what you are seeking. Enduring the pain enables the finding."

Jude responded, "I know, we've talked about this. Logically I understand, but the feelings can be tortuous."

"You have endured those feelings for the last several years. You've been courageous in your quest to feel whole," Father Pratt proudly said. "Your guidance has been so important." Jude responded welling up.

Early in Jude's therapy Father Pratt realized that Jude was exceptionally bright and deeply aware of his feelings. Over time, Jude's therapy has explored his unconscious and viewed the ordinary through multi-colored prisms. Over and above those vistas, Jude has known that living in the present, while looking to the past, helps shape the future. But despite those insights, his work is not without painful doubts and challenges—for after all, it is psychotherapy. Father Pratt has supported him in weathering those difficult times.

Jude has deeply yearned to integrate his experiences and his beliefs, but success has been elusive. Nevertheless, he has forged on, focusing on his most uncomfortable feelings. Jude has held on to hope and faith, believing he will find his centermost self.

Father Pratt has reassured him, "Trust the process, time will reveal your direction."

Jude was born in a small American state. His mother, a devout Christian, embraces her religion with open arms. Whether with the mundane details of life or her deepest experiences, Jesus is woven into her thoughts, feelings and actions. Christ the Lord is at the center of her existence. He is always with her.

Jude's father, a physicist, relies on logic and empirical evidence to organize and define reality. Whether it's a staggering mathematical formula, or numbers from daily life, he is tuned in by way of calculations. His understanding of the universe has been at the cutting edge for many years. People such as Albert Einstein, Neils Bohr, Werner Heisenberg and Paul Dirac were essentially his workmates at the corner of Universe Parkway and Black Hole Boulevard. Although Jude's father followed life's course through numbers, his devotion to his family has been without fail.

Growing up, Jude was not for want. His parents did not lack money, nor were they parsimonious with their loving support. Jude was encouraged to seek his own contribution to the journey of mankind. A long history of high achievers dotted the family tree on both ancestral lines.

Since a young boy, Jude has shown a natural confidence relating to others. In his formative years, Jude developed an inordinate capacity for concentration and invention. He was always creating something clever, whether with words, an image, or an object. Often he captured an ethereal expression relating to an instant in time.

But despite successes, he never boasted, nor was he full of himself. In his heart of hearts, Jude fully appreciated the beauty and value of every human being. He considered this a wonderful gift, lovingly placed inside him by the caring hands of his parents. For this, his gratitude was endless.

Jude has always had a deep admiration for his mother's devotion to her personal savior, Jesus Christ the Lord. As a young boy, she faithfully read him the Bible every night filling him with the history of Jesus' time. Over time, Jude's curiosity led to many questions about Christ, His followers, and those who reportedly wrote the Bible.

But despite his intense interest, Jude's parents decided he would attend a secular school. This gave objectivity a boost, as they were concerned that the ritualistic cloak of a non-secular school might dampen his natural interest and muddy the waters of his fine intellect.

Jude and his father shared an affinity for science and mathematics. They applied their interests to the smallest of small, i.e. sub-atomic theory, and the largest of large, the study of cosmology.

Jude was particularly drawn to time, which both intrigued *and* haunted him. His free imagination provided an enormous capacity for meditative direction. Bottomless ravines of time and existence were contemplated by his navigable courage. His exploration knew no bounds, as he could shift from complex mathematical formulas, to understanding the fabric of a feeling.

Although there was a major chasm between his parents' belief systems, they got along surprisingly well. Their practice of making decisions together, and living their lives in a shared manner, solidified their family. Their disparate views did not cause family discord in any manner.

But their innately different weltanschauung left a divided impression upon Jude. Although he loved his parents, he struggled to unite their worlds within him. Through therapy Jude sought to weave two rich tapestries into one. Yes, he could entertain both poles of vision, but the wish to create a transcending reality burned deeply within. Without a union he was not whole.

Jude traveled to the Holy Land, first one visit, then another and another. Each time he became more intensely attuned to the life and travels of Jesus Christ. All the while he's been at graduate school studying his dual majors of Physics and the languages of Jesus' era, that being Aramaic and Hebrew.

Many an hour he imagined the time of Jesus and how recently He walked upon the earth. Considering how long mankind has existed, Jesus was *just here.* Jude *just* missed Him.

He lamented not having lived in the Holy Land at the time of Christ. If he had, he would have sought answers to certain longstanding questions: "Did Jesus truly exist? Is He the miracle performing Son of God? If not, is he the biggest imposter who ever lived or simply a man who others attached fantastic stories to? If Jesus is not the Son of God, who or what is at the heart of existence? Is reality simply an astronomically complex series of interfacing matter and energy explainable by scientific laws?"

Glaring was the gulf in Jude, as he thought of his mother's blind faith and how his father would not, could not, recognize anything that wasn't measurable. Deeply unsettling, these possibilities collided within, seeking internal resolution. This conflict was most pointedly *the* contributing factor that brought Jude to see a professional.

Father Pratt was a licensed Psychotherapist as well as an ordained Priest. This was not coincidental, as Jude wanted a person of faith, as well as a scientist. Father Pratt's spiritual beliefs, coupled with his scientific knowledge of psychological processes, united the separate aspects of his being. Jude looked up to Father Pratt for having successfully integrated his heart and mind by helping others adapt to a challenging world.

From the first session forward, empathic treatment created a safe atmosphere where Jude allowed Father Pratt to peer deep inside his mind. Two trusted as one.

Jude spoke early of wishes. Father Pratt respectfully highlighted the differences between wishes that are attainable and those that are designed to provide hope or self-cohesion. But despite this clarification, Jude continued to seek the sought, divorced from whether his wishes could or would be realized.

Then, one peaceful Sunday morning, life for Jude changed forever. A drunk driver killed his best friend. This was followed by a health scare for Jude's father. These two occurrences led to Jude grieving and projecting the loss of his parents. This in turn, left Jude contemplating his own mortality. It was a most difficult time.

Although Jude shared his feelings in therapy for several months, he began to withdraw from others. His enthusiasm in the immediate world diminished, as he lost interest in daily chores and faded into himself.

Despite appearing to be clinically depressed, neither Father Pratt, nor Jude, wanted to label his experience as a "disorder."

Both trusted in Jude's free-range of feelings and his comfort with internal contradictions.

Soon after, Jude told Father Pratt of his wish to work on issues alone. Father Pratt was torn, but after exploration knew to respect Jude's wish. Having talked of his feelings, Jude shifted, choosing his analytic self, partly for emotional relief, partly to seek higher ground. Jude decided the timing was right to pursue a complex mathematical project he'd been contemplating.

After asking his parents for the use of a far-down-the-road-barn, he isolated himself in its stable, where his work was born.

For Jude, it was a time of immense focus in a wilderness of his own. He became less and less relatable as numbers became the draw of his attention. Deep into the black realm of calculations he dove. His solitariness grew exponentially, as his world turned cold. Starkly bare correctness scraped the sky, as he timelessly passed through empty streets of nowhere and no one. His world consisted of exact and unyielding numbers, juxtaposed with an emptiness of immeasurable proportions. Stone cold pillars stretched endlessly tall, screeching in their deafening silence.

Inhabiting this world made Jude feel non-existent. But he held on, seeking the number relationship. At the bottom, the puzzle piece fit, 0 equaled 0. He withdrew from being withdrawn and contacted Father Pratt. After nearly 6 weeks, Father Pratt's belief in Jude had not wavered. Nonetheless, he was relieved to hear from him. Father Pratt saw him that same day. Jude looked quite tired.

"How are you?" Father Pratt asked as he scanned Jude's appearance.

"I'm ok. Very tired though. I've never had such an experience."

"What was it like?"

"Hard to reflect on it at the moment, Father, I'm pulling myself away from that state of mind. I need to focus on the here and now, so I don't fall back into the world of computation. It took some doing to leave there and be here. Just driving my car required tremendous focus, as it felt so alien."

"Wow," Father Pratt said, nearly whispering. "What else?" he asked of Jude.

"My project has revived my feelings. Yet the time alone was very punishing. I now know, what it's like to be mad."

Father Pratt sat back as a still silence subdued the room.

Jude comfortably broke it. "Having said that, I can assure you I'm okay. As we meet I'll share more about my last 6 weeks. But for now I wish to readapt to present day. You've probably noticed that I lost a considerable amount of weight. I tried to meet my nutritional needs, but fell short. My immediate goal is to replenish my overall health."

"That sounds wise Jude," Father Pratt said quietly.

"Father, I understand the importance of keeping the clinical frame. Meeting twice a week for 6 weeks will help me acclimate to life outside of mathematical calculations."

"Yes," Father Pratt responded.

Having plumbed the depths of his analytic self, Jude reengaged, which of course included Jesus. Over the next few weeks Jude quickly regained his physical, mental and emotional equilibrium. In fact, he felt more confident and knowledgeable than ever before. Father Pratt was pleased to see that Jude's experience in the wilderness strengthened him. Still though, Jude sought the ever elusive solution to cure the cleave within.

Then one early winter morning, pieces flashed together. His brainchild sprang to mind, secured by a hook through his heart. A union was born.

However curious, the realization came as he began the 4th year of his 4th decade. A perfect time for heart and mind to unite! Jude diligently applied the final components to his ambitious and outrageous venture.

As his next session approached, Jude grew eager to tell Father Pratt that his wish had transformed to a plan. He showed on time as usual.

"*Hey Jude*, how are you?"

"Hi Father, I'm fine. I want to talk with you about a few things."

"Oh?"

Jude looked at the floor as he said, "I've been thinking a lot about Jesus."

They both paused before Father Pratt asked, "Do you mean more than usual? He's been on your mind for some time."

"Yes, more than usual."

"What is going on for you?" Father Pratt queried.

"I'm obsessed with him, but I can't say why."

"Jude, do you think your preoccupation with Jesus relates to those difficult emotions you've been feeling?"

Jude paused. "I'm sure you're right, as my waking day is peppered with images, thoughts and feelings about Christ. On some level, I imagine they're meant to compensate for the emptiness, but there's a shift since my reverie."

Father Pratt leaned forward and asked, "Jude, is it dichotomous, where either you feel empty and alone, or feel you're losing yourself in Christ?"

"No, not that polar, although there are some common threads to what you're saying, I have found a middle ground. Jesus is on my mind because I'm immersed with my plan, my journey for...well you know the term, self-actualization. I'm on the road to unite my halves and be whole."

"Oh?" Father Pratt responded, containing his personal curiosity and concern. "How is it getting close to your goal?"

"Well, there are a myriad of feelings."

"What can you say about it?" Father Pratt asked.

"Father, I am sorry, I cannot yet reveal about my journey. I know it's not healthy to keep secrets, but you'll have to trust me. I can't say anything more."

"I believe there's a misunderstanding. I was asking how you felt about being close to your goal, not the specifics of it."

"Oh, I'm sorry. I guess I'm being overly protective of my plans," Jude said apologetically.

Father Pratt was sympathetic. "It seems so. So let's talk about nearing your objective without concern I might circumnavigate to seek your secret. But first, let me ask you. Where did that misunderstanding come from?"

Jude felt badly, but forgave himself immediately revealing, "I am now following a clear direction. But the path has its risks and I'm imagining the possibilities."

Jude took a breath. "There are several outcomes possible. Independent of whether I am successful, there's a chance I could run out of time or not survive."

Father Pratt forced the question from his lips. "You could lose your life?"

"Yes, Father, that is a possibility."

"I want to respect whatever plan you've devised, yet I'm not certain how to respond to the idea you may not survive."

Silence.

Father Pratt continued. "Knowing you, it seems to me you'd only risk your life, if it were truly important."

"Yes Father, I love life and wouldn't chance it unless it was for a higher purpose. This is the way. I am seeking the truth. I am following the light. It is my calling, my destiny."

Father Pratt was shaken, "Your destiny? I've never heard you speak so fatefully."

Jude nodded his head.

"Since this could lead to your death, will you promise to talk more before deciding to act?"

"Yes, I promise," Jude said with commitment. "That's reassuring, thank you."

Silence.

Father Pratt intuitively knew to shift back to the process. "Apart from your rationale, I imagine you know that withholding a secret can limit my helping. That said, I am not pushing you to share more today, I am only making it clear what you are creating between us."

Silence.

Father Pratt added, "I wonder if it's similar to you withholding contradictions between your parents, protecting each from the others' world."

"Perhaps," Jude answered, "but as you'll soon know, my project is complex. It has innumerable outcomes, which could impact not only me, but the entire world. I have to contain and direct the project from start to finish to avoid unintended developments. I need to be deliberate and controlled. I've not come this far to be reckless out of anticipatory excitement or poor judgment. As well, I'm anxious about achieving success."

"Anxious about success?"

"As far as I see, success validates one reality and rules out the other. Even though it's what I've been seeking, it's scary to consider. The co-existing worlds within me will no longer receive equal billing. One will be accepted, the other rejected. Yet, paradoxically, I seek a union."

Father Pratt was never more curious. "If I understand you, the worldview of your mother and father that exists within you, will be reconciled, yes?"

"Yes, Father, that's exactly right."

Father Pratt added, "The large of your work contains the wish to be whole, uniting both faith and reason. Jesus seems to be the calm center of that effort."

"Yes, I am seeking the center. I'm looking for the bright light of truth hidden in the vague shade of 2000 years."

Silence prevailed as Father Pratt looked at Jude with veneration.

He then asked, "If questions are answered, are you concerned about your parents or the balance within yourself?"

"I have to give that some thought, but I see we're out of time." Jude said.

"Yes, we are," said Father Pratt hiding his own disappointment.

There are no shortcuts in preparation for extensive barefoot walking. So for now, Jude's comfortable running shoes were left in the closet. He walked often, paying careful attention to not cut or injure his feet, as an injury could delay his plan.

Having Mediterranean features naturally suited Jude for his endeavor. Adding a beard to his shoulder length hair furthered his cause. Jude had bought period clothing at his last pilgrimage to the Holy Land. In addition, he accumulated the actual coin of Jesus' era by buying them on eBay.

As his future was drained of its wait, he recalled the Boy Scouts adage from all those years ago, "Be Prepared."

Jude reflected on the path that lay before him. The only remaining factor in realizing his wish was the attestation of his calculations. Feeling tall, Jude walked with conviction to the old farm buildings that housed his dwelling.

The time had come to test it. The numbers had been worked out in meticulous detail. Years of contemplation and calculation occurred before a key insight led to its creation.

Jude mused, "Although I created it, I might not believe my own eyes. Imagine, a Device that can travel through time! Will this be the vehicle that shines light on my vexing questions?"

After all the wishes, all the thoughts and all the work, he wondered how accurately he'd be in placing it when and where he desired. Jude smiled as he welcomed the thought, *"Time has come today."*

So the day before he was going to test his Device by sending it back in time a day, Jude went to the location he would be sending it to tomorrow and was pleased to find it today, right where he was going to send it!

He then set the calculations for it to go forward in time to tomorrow and had it arrive seconds after he'll send it to today.

Although Jude was delighted his Device worked, its success committed him to a reality previously only imagined. Now, there was no turning back.

He attended his next appointment with thoughtful concern. "Father, I've thought more about your question. I am mostly concerned about my parents, particularly my *mother*. Both my parents are tightly secured to their belief system, so whatever truth I may discover could affect them."

Father Pratt quietly nodded.

Jude continued, "But it is up to me if I share it. They protected me during my formative years, so if indicated, I'll do the same for them. My well-being is an entirely different topic."

"I see," Father Pratt said, realizing the wealth of directions opened up by Jude.

Jude's words flowed further, "I fully accept how ever the project turns out. As they say, "One is responsible for the effort, but not the outcome.""

Father Pratt responded shaking his head yes, "I understand."
"Father, I am also concerned about you."

"About me? In what way?"

"If this plan does not work out, I don't want you to blame yourself. You are an excellent therapist, you deserve to feel proud of your work, regardless of the result."

"Thank you for your kind thoughts," Father Pratt said. "You've been tirelessly dedicated to your therapy. You have a fathomless heart and a remarkable intellect. I respect you regardless of the outcome. Whatever your plan is, I truly believe you'll be successful."

"Thank you Father. Now I'll share the details of my journey. But first, let me ask you. Is a miracle performed by a machine any more unlikely to consider than one by a human being?"

Father Pratt answered from a thinking place, as he waited for the emotional surprise, "Apparently not in your eyes, since you're asking me this question. I'm assuming that you're talking about Jesus and the miracles He performed?"

"Yes, I am," Jude said flatly.

A suggestion of excitement appeared in Father Pratt's tone, "Are you suggesting you've invented a machine that can perform miracles? If a machine could accomplish a miracle, then it would no longer be considered a miracle."

"What do you mean?" Jude asked.

"Well, if 200 years ago someone had talked outloud with another person from a distance of one hundred miles, it would be considered a miracle. But when the telephone was invented, talking at that distance would no longer be considered a miracle."

"You're absolutely right, Father."

Father Pratt could stand it no longer, "What have you created Jude?"

"I have created a Device that can travel in Time."

Father Pratt was incredulous, "What? You've made a Time Machine? *A Real Time Machine?* Have you tried it? Where, or more importantly, when are you traveling to?"

Jude replied without hesitation, "I'm going to travel back in time, 2000 years. I am going on a pilgrimage to look for Jesus. I will seek to verify His existence and establish if He is truly the Son of God."

"Oh my God Jude."

"You shouldn't take the Lord's name in vain, Father."

Over the next 7 weeks, Jude and Father Pratt talked about the many details of his endeavor. They also discussed potential outcomes such as Jude becoming trapped in another time.

Woven into the sessions were reflections of their work and the possibility of it coming to an end.

Their last session came quickly. Precisely at the usual time Father Pratt opened his door to find Jude patiently waiting, having just arrived. They both quietly noted their mirror-like movements as they sat in unison. Tears brimmed, but none flowed, as they talked warmly of their relationship, but maintained the professionalism they had always had. They highlighted the valuable, the memorable, the humorous and the meaningful.

With a few minutes left, Jude welled up, "The most generous gift from our work is *knowing* authentic beauty is offered in every moment. It's in our eyes to see and our hearts to feel. You, Father Pratt, have shown me a way."

Silence filled the room, as their hearts beat in time.

Then, practicality emerged as Jude signed a confidential release allowing Father Pratt to share with Jude's parents the details of the undertaking. The release was clear, "Any and all information about the treatment of Jude K. Pasternak."

A few words of affection were shared as they warmly shook hands goodbye. There was a surreal feel as they both felt it was a final adieu.

The door was then closed.

Saying goodbye to his parents came *way* too quickly. They arranged to meet on a strip of sand bordering the ocean's edge. His parents parked at the north end of the beach, Jude the south. Arriving together in time, each appeared as a dot on the beach in the far, far distance. As they walked toward one another, fears and wishes surged within. Crashing waves punctuated every step as their images swelled from tiny, to the reality of close. Upon meeting, wordless hugs were followed by 6 eyes scanning the sand for nothing known, nor desired. Since Jude had shared he was working on a plan of significance, his parents anticipated they might be saying goodbye. Jude's serious mood added sizable weight to the moment. Jude proceeded without hesitancy. "I am soon to be embarking upon a great journey, not dissimilar to the sailors who voyaged uncharted seas of the 15th Century."

He continued without waiting for a response, "This is a high-risk undertaking that offers no guarantee for my safety and could conceivably end my life."

Wide-eyed, tear streamed silence shook the air. Time froze, as Jude and his parents felt unimaginable loss hovering at the height of their hearts.

Jude apologetically said, "'I'm sorry about the risk, but it is time. Both of you know I've been seeking truth. This journey is my quest. I'm so sorry that I cannot share more."

His parents knew by words and countenance that this was the most important decision of his life. His mother felt the courage flaming in his heart, while his father estimated the extent of his son's vision.

"We love you Jude. You know your father and I fully support your journey. It's difficult to not know more, but you'll not be alone, Jesus will be with you."

Jude's father added, "Yes, we love you and I'm positive that whatever calculations you've made for your journey are exactly correct. For that I am certain."

"Thanks Mom, Dad, you've always been there for me." With tears Jude fell in a well of love. Bleeding with feeling, he said, "I love you forevermore."

Extensive hugs gladdened their sad hearts. Jude brought them back to words. "Father Pratt will share the details of my venture in Time."

When Jude shared that he had donated sperm at a CryoBank, his parents' initial surprise quickly shifted to alarm, as they wondered about his chances to return.

In fact, Jude was *also* concerned, hence he was leaving a genetic legacy should his risky trek not work out. He withheld confirming their fear, instead talking of the science of double helix DNA and how two strands chemically bind. Diverting from further anguish, he shared the good news that three mothers were each soon to have a child of his! Jude was to become a father to three! This unexpected news shook them up. But, the fact that Jude had arranged full grandparent rights left them deeply pleased. The three of them shared bittersweet congratulations.

The afternoon became short, as preparations needed tending to. After all the words and all the tears there were more hugs, followed by the painful walking away. Longing took hold as their attempts to resist looking back were to no avail. As the sand and sky swallowed them from sight, each imagined the mast of an old sailing ship disappearing last on the ocean horizon.

Jude's Mom went and prayed, as his Dad calculated a risk assessment using general laws of probability.

Jude proceeded with his plan. Early the next day, he rose after a night of restful sleep. He collected his belongings and walked 880 yards to the stable where his journey was to be born. The sun was bright and the blue sky was like a dome containing the unending— until this morning—moment of now.

Jude approached his vehicle with a full respect for the God who allowed its creation. He recognized that his Device was ultimately a refusal to accept reality as it was known. Jude knew if successful, he was joining a long list of revolutionaries whose vision and courage changed the world forever. Luminaries such as Nicolaus Copernicus, Issac Newton and Sigmund Freud opened up endless doors of knowing by challenging customary norms, beliefs, and societal structure.

Although Jude was intrigued by time and its constancy, he felt trapped by its control. These feelings were mollified by the knowledge that all life is enslaved to the sliver of time between what has happened and what will happen. Like the relentless second hand of a clock, time chases the future, while racing from the past.

But now it is the past that Jude is chasing and he has the means to do so. Never before had there been a choice. Jude was now prepared to escape from the ultimate confinement, the bonds of Time.

Sliding the barn door open revealed shafts of sunlight slicing the air, lighting up lines on his tunic. Serenely respecting the moment, Jude gently sat upon his Device.

Knowing the risks he was taking, Jude took a deep breath and looked longingly at the immediate world. He mentally checked his list of takes and had them all.

Then, with rock hard resolve, Jude pushed his Device forward into the past. Seconds ticked by with a whirl, as a shrill pitch grew in intensity. His heart beat faster and faster as it fought to keep pace. Jude recalled Neil Armstrong's warp-speed pulse rate during the first moon landing some 50 years before. Calculating brought a smile, as the first man on the moon—in minute's time—won't be born for *2000 years!*

"Yikes!" he muttered.

Seconds felt like hours, yet in truth, centuries were passing by in minutes!

Suddenly, with a jolt, Jude arrived at his destination. Shook up and disoriented, he called upon his faculties, holding in abeyance any reaction until knowing his status.

Still reeling from his journey, he stepped to the outer edge of the cave to evaluate his immediate place and time. Although he quickly concluded he had arrived at the cave of his design, he observed the Sun's position and deduced by instrument that he had undershot time by a great number of months. Knowing if he were to be seen, it could complicate situations in unexpected ways, Jude directly removed himself back to his Device. He hoped that the woman he had caught a glimpse of had not seen him.

Jude recalibrated his traveling Device and was right on after a second attempt. The second trip was just a step compared to the marathon he endured "minutes" before.

Jude cautiously ventured from the cave, securing his Device by maneuvering a large rock to block the cave entrance.

Looking beyond the immediate area he saw people dressed in the period's conventional garb. This sight released any celebratory resistance he was holding, as his body soared with delight! The Holy Land of the First Century lay before his eyes! Arriving at this time and place in history was beyond comprehension. Elated beyond words, each beat of his heart surged a deep thrill through his body, while the center of his being shook hands with itself.

"I did it!" Jude exclaimed. However, his celebration of self was fleeting, as he didn't indulge in self-aggrandizement.

Much can be said about Jude's time in the Holy Land 2000 years ago. With perfect regularity Jude woke each morning to a sparkling mix of intoxicating excitement, freshly provided by the fruits of his labor. Each step taken was alternatively met with disbelief, then exultation! Powerful feelings intermittently coursed through his body. As he moved forward in his travels, he felt suspended, floating above the world.

Jude imagined he knew how Vasco da Gama, Ferdinand Magellan and other explorers felt during their adventures. Yet, Jude mused, they looked forward to the New World, while he's looking backward to the Old World. Jude noted that Charles Lindbergh and Amelia Earhart also traveled a solitary sojourn. But others knew about their adventures. Except for Father Pratt who was 2000 years away, no one knew of Jude's real identity, or his quest. This led him to feel detached and inexorably alone. With Father Pratt in his thoughts, Jude yielded to the deep sting of *those* feelings.

Although prepared by learning the languages and customs of the time, it was still daunting to be in the ancient Holy Land concealing an incomprehensible secret. In the interests of coping, Jude applied his flowing knowing to feel the shifting real of here and now.

After several days, Jude knew it was time for his mission. He thought, "Yes, I have found a *key* hole in the door of Time. The immutable wall to the past has been pierced! Yet, my divide yearns for oneness."

He looked at the horizon, "Let me find Him...I have come this far, let me find Him." His words echoed through his being.

It was Jude's plan to seek Jesus where He was known to have walked. Jude's knowledge of Jesus' time and the Holy Land was of great value. In addition, his empathic skills aided interaction with others, helping insure his freedom of travel.

Jude decided to begin at the beginning, so he began his trek to Bethlehem. He quickly learned the difference between knowing there is no mass transit and experiencing it, as the walking wore on him.

As he proceeded, he looked for and asked about Jesus. After many miles he had to admit a sense of initial disappointment, as no one knew of Him.

Some weeks later, Jude reached Bethlehem anticipating that many would know of Christ. But not only was there no knowledge of Jesus, Jude curiously found himself telling the beautiful and moving report of Christ Jesus' birth to the townspeople, who were quite taken by the account. A warm exchange was witnessed as Jude moved ahead with his quest.

But as Jude continued to walk in the footprints of Jesus he was mystified that there continued to be no recognition of Christ the Lord.

Jude believed he was accurate with his calculations and felt confident he had come to the right place, at the right time, yet wondered if after 2000 years, some of the reported "facts" had been altered, like in a child's circle game of "telephone."

However, not all of Jude's efforts were for naught, as a smattering of people had heard of John The Baptist. This solidified Jude's reckoning with Time.

Several months later as Jude was walking north toward Nazareth, he yielded to his sore feet and sought relief in the restorative waters of the Sea of Galilee. Jude took the opportunity to share more of Christ's message of love with the hope that others may have heard it.

But, only his feet were soothed, as his efforts to confirm Jesus as the Savior were stymied. Nonetheless, those who heard Jude responded well to Jesus' words, as the ground was fertile for love.

After some months Jude began to recognize several young men who appeared to be shadowing him. Over time Jude noted their increased numbers and their apparent interest in learning more of Christ. Although they seemed to be genuine, Jude recalled his Bible studies and how betrayal in the Holy Land had been problematic, hence he remained cautious.

However, it was more than Jesus' words that raised an interest in Jude. His standing among the people rose considerably when Jude saved the life—by way of CPR—of a man believed to be dead.

Over many, many months Jude continued to seek Jesus. Although discouraged, he continued to believe Christ would emerge. While time passed, Jude embraced the beauty of the people and their customs. Daily life offered a sweet richness that Jude did not overlook.

Some time later, at a grassy place east of the Jordan River near Bethsaida, Jude's recounting of Jesus' message attracted a multitude of people. Love filled the listeners as Jude recited Christ's words. Many became generous of heart, sharing their bread and fish with others. Jude was moved by the power of God's word, yet felt a deepening sense of loss, having not found the Prince of Peace, the Lord Jesus Christ. Nor did he find a man who could account for Christianity.

The more Jude spoke, the more uncomfortable he became. Having a sophisticated understanding of the political climate of the era, Jude became concerned that the Romans and other political factions were watching him.

Then one day, Jude's fear was realized. Roman Soldiers sought Jude out and arrested him in an aggressive manner. Although they had questions about this person Jesus, they focused intensely on Jude. As time pressed on, Jude realized his natural ability to win people over was powerfully outweighed by the strong arm of the Romans. Although he considered escaping, there was no opportunity to do so. Jude had decided a long time ago, back in the future, that he would never tell anyone about his mission. He was not willing to chance affecting history any more than he may already have.

Then, Jude's grim situation escalated to grave, as he was sentenced to death. Beat to the edge of his life, Jude had to endure what his subject of interest had suffered, carrying a wooden cross across a long distance.

As he struggled along, Jude felt entirely alone in a state of total disconnect. He had spent several years living an unbelievable dream but now found himself in disbelief about a reality too painful to deny. Each labored step convinced him further of his imminent death. Jude's past was now very far away. A pall of failure engrossed his being. He searched desperately for a comforting thought from Father Pratt, but to no avail. Even the Father's statement about the value of disconnection and emptiness did not offer solace.

"I am all alone. Soon, I am going to die alone. I have no one. I have failed. My past in the future will never be present again. My parents will never know the outcome of my life. Father Pratt will never again soothe my anguish. What is this about? Is there a value to this suffering that I can't see? Am I failing to have faith and believe?"

Still carrying the cross, Jude stumbled, struggling to stay on his feet. He then came upon a place that sent shivers up his spine. Jude recognized the area from past tours of the Holy Land, taken years ago in the future. This is where crucifixions occurred. This is where Jesus was put to death.

Following orders, Jude laid down, as his hands and feet were nailed to the cross. Despite the intense pain, he thought of the irony,

"I invent a machine and travel 20 centuries to find Christ and there's no sign He ever existed. And now I'm going to die as He reportedly did, through crucifixion!"

Jude felt lost and profoundly alone. Feelings of betrayal shifted to shame, as his life appeared meaningless. As he was raised with the others into a vertical position, the pain became utterly intolerable. Then, suddenly, his suffering fell away as his body powerfully shook and a blinding light burst through him.

"Oh my God, in Heaven, I am the Jesus, I am the Savior! I am the Christ figure who was written about! His words were really my words that I got from him, shaped by 2000 years of telling."

Lifting his head, his view was unveiled. An immense wave of love poured into his heart as he imagined the billions of people receiving comfort and direction in their lives, because he sacrificed his for them.

Jude remained immersed in a timeless glow of love, as he ardently imagined telling his mother, "I was there as the nails were hammered into the Christ figures' hands and feet. I was there as the cross was raised. I felt his pain and had a sense of oneness with him more than I can say." Jude knew his mother would be unendingly proud of him.

Jude knew his father would understand his sacrifice. Billions of lives are more important than just *one solitary life.* Jude imagined telling him, "You can be certain that our effort to define what is real, is now perfectly clear."

Jude held these words in his heart, "Father Pratt, I've never felt so alone, yet so filled with love. Both exist. The light and the night..."

Jude's pain-wracked existence held on. Looking at the sky, the earth, and those in view, he mustered these last few words, "My destiny is here...united truths...love for all...in all Time...here in *paradise.*"

Moments later, a Roman Soldier on horseback stabbed Jude in the side, shedding his rich red blood for millenniums to come.

Nothing definitive can be said regarding his burial place as historical details conflict. Notwithstanding, on the third day following the crucifixion, a microchip reading of Jude's death triggered his Device to self-destruct. The explosive force rolled away the stone.

That same day, Jude appeared in the cave. He came to the cave entrance before retiring swiftly back to his Device.

This sighting initially confused Mary Magdalene. As she proceeded to explore the cave further, the low whirling sound of the Device could not be heard, as it and its occupant disappeared into the light.

THE END

Theatre Of The Empathic

CHAPTER 1

Thriving green shrubbery tightly cling to the edge of the downward winding road. Houses pop, dotting the landscape with perpendicular lines and lively colors. Changing shapes pleasingly flow as the sun casts pre-dusk shadows upon the forms. The city lies below, nestled between a long mountain ridge and Loon Lake.

It was as if the general population followed Aldous Huxley and ingested a daily dose of soma. A general air of tranquility between man and his neighbor replaced centuries of dissension. Discord and strife melted away, yielding to a descending calm in both village and countryside, as the incidence of violent crimes was reduced 92%.

Yes, there were occasional disagreements, but civility reigned as a general rule. Divorce rates plunged to near nonexistent. Chemical addiction bottomed out, challenging the disease concept as nurture took a front seat in causation. Medical costs tumbled, as health overwhelmingly superseded illness, creating happier and more integrated citizens.

Predictably, the demand for lawyers plummeted, as conflicts were easily resolved. Psychotherapists, instrumental in supporting this metamorphosis, have all but driven themselves out of business, as serenity embodied the general public. Competitive strivings were tamed by common purpose, as the society of man was likened to honeybees, working for the benefit of the hive. Major societal changes have been accomplished, one person at a time.

CHAPTER 2

There was nothing outstanding or unusual about the theatre that night. It was your standard movie theater built in the mid 20th century. A stage stands where the screen once hung. It was

Saturday night and the patrons were excitedly streaming in to find an open seat. Smiles were everywhere as stranger spoke to stranger, eagerly connecting to the new and true of the other.

Jordana stood trembling behind the curtain. In mere moments, she would be called to step center stage. Being aware of the impending value did not lessen her anxiety.

She wondered, "Can I do this? Will the audience understand? Will it work for me?"

As per the tradition of "The Theatre," each speaker is allotted two back-to-back periods of 47 minutes to share his or her life passage.

The audience listens non-judgmentally while conveying a caring attunement to the events and choices of the speaker's life. Accomplishments are admired, as oohs and aahs are punctuated with the smiles and tears of empathic compassion. They feel the speakers' losses and pain, while forgiving the missteps and sharing the joys. The audience believes, without reservation, that *just surviving is a noble cause.* Their sincerity is unmistakable as sentiments flow between their hearts and the heart of the speaker.

Empathic connection is forged by authentic expression and genuine receptivity. Within that truth the parties are in harmony. The Theatre experience melts away hurt, anger, guilt and confusion buried deep inside. Even those of fiery temperament are struck with a peaceful countenance and a stability relating with others. At times, an experience of magical wonder took hold as boundaries blurred into oceanic oneness. Lives became transformed, as many reported feeling truly whole for the first time.

Over time, many in society embraced "The Theatre of The Empathic," as having a curative influence rivaling any other therapy or self-help program. Although a few non-believers referred to it as mass hypnosis, their numbers diminished daily. Even if that were so, it would not detract from the positive effect the Theatre has had on those who share. No one could devalue the healing power of sharing their life with 350 compassionate strangers.

When Jordana's moment finally arrived, the rising curtain exposed the kind faces that ringed the room. Jordana quickly fell into a well of comfort, as she shared her life story. Words and feelings flowed with ease, just as they did for those before her.

It went predictably well, evidenced by Jordana's beaming face. She gracefully bowed to the audience, appreciating their thunderous praise.

CHAPTER 3

Like many large-scale movements, an unexpected moment revealed a direction that defined a future. The Theatre's genesis was a middle school class flagged for bullying after a substitute teacher lost control of his class.

So on that fateful morning in April, 17 years ago, a School Social Worker, Miss Hatcher, returned to her class and initiated an experiential exercise. To start, she engaged her students in defining empathy. Then she called upon a brave young lady to be the first. Miss Hatcher asked the students to empathetically be in tune with Eve, as she shared an overview of her life.

"Imagine," Miss Hatcher said, "what it's like to be Eve. Do your best to not judge what she says, or how she says it. Just feel her world, as if it were your own."

At first, the class was tentative, but Miss Hatcher capitalized on established trust and gently guided them through the activity. Eve reported feeling "great" following the experience.

By late morning other students had stepped up and shared, receiving in turn, an attentive and enthusiastic response from the class. Week's later, parents of those who shared spoke of the positive changes in their children's behavior and disposition.

Since Miss Hatcher continued to succeed, the Principal approved the exercise for other classes. Slowly but steadily, the empathic experience spread.

Pleased by its broad acceptance, Miss Hatcher promoted it with students of continuing education classes. She was quickly delighted to see adults have such a positive response!

Success raised her curiosity, as she wondered why this exercise was so transformational.

Over time, she developed a treatise providing the theoretical underside of the empathic experience. This offered credence to decision makers who considered this exercise for their constituencies. In addition, talk around the community raised awareness, increasing those who wanted to share.

When the media covered the empathic phenomenon, its popularity broadened further still, resulting in Church and State institutions signing on. It became clear that society had a deep hunger for spiritual connection. Politics, education and the world of entertainment increasingly viewed life through the lens of empathic sensitivity.

The popularity of breaking customary cultural norms to shock for attention or monetary **ga**in slipped away, as superficial notoriety became stale and meaningless.

Momentum accelerated exponentially, as empathic structure attached to existing convention and rules of conduct. Society became engulfed as empathic attunement became the rave. As the movement progressed, an eye-opening awareness grew like vines in a rain forest. The wonder and brilliance of "screens," so prolific from their beginnings in the early 1900's, were now seen in a different light. It became clear that a gulf existed between people, in part, due to the ubiquitous use of devices.

Yes, screen time offers connection by way of smart phones, watches and computers, as well as television and live video. They provide news, movies, music, photos, games, books, voting, business and social exchanges of varied forms. Yet, screens act as a barrier that clouds closeness between people.

As the social tide turned, the status of screens was left gasping for air, as a tsunami of real bonding flooded in. Nothing could compete with looking into the eyes of another person, feeling their feelings and thinking their thoughts.

No, screens did not cease to exist, but rather took their deserved position in society as an aid to connection, not *the* connection.

In a smattering of years, the practice of empathic attunement had unexpectedly emerged from an ordinary seventh grade class to be the central guiding doctrine of society.

CHAPTER 4

This is not to suggest that empathy was born on that notable April morning. For without empathic attunement mankind wouldn't have survived from our beginnings to present day. However, with the recent mindful application of empathic engagement an evolutionary leap has been forged, transforming man and society forever forward. The igniting catalyst leading to this movement had its origins with Miss Hatcher and Eve. All these years later, Miss Hatcher, now a married Mrs. Ubergang, is still quite involved with the Empathic Movement. Because the prismatic point of empathy is an application relevant to any human endeavor, Mrs. Ubergang founded the University Of Empathic Studies. The course curriculum was designed to enrich and amplify the capacity for empathy.

The following are some of the courses offered:

SUSPENDING JUDGMENT AS AN AGENT FOR OPENNESS 101
NARCISSISTIC INCARCERATION: A HARSH SENTENCE 101
NARCISSISTIC NARROWING OF EXPERIENCE: INHERENTLY WOEFUL 101
PROJECTING IMAGINATIVE EXPERIENCE INTO ANTS 101
OPPOSITES MAKE A WHOLE 200
SHARPENED EDGES, ROUNDED CORNERS: EMBRACING THE SHAPE 200
DEEPENING THE HEART 201
INTUITION: ESSENTIAL 300
COMMON DETAILS AND THEIR IMPACT UPON EMPATHIC ACCURACY 200
MOVING IN THE PRESENT 300

CHAPTER 5

But despite success, empathic failures were unavoidable. Although society is resigned to their existence, active efforts are put forth to reduce them.

This is the mission of the Empathic Enforcers. The "EE" as they are known, patrol the Theatre looking for those indifferent or detached from the speaker. Infractors are singled out and ticketed for breach of empathic connection.

Since studies determine that a high incidence of empathic connection coincides with an appreciation for aesthetic beauty, classes of mandated cloud watching are assigned to those guilty of an empathic failure. A second infraction is more serious, calling for the individual to paint 30 sunsets, in 30 days, watercolor or oil accepted.

As the Theatre became an established part of society, a strange development occurred.

Serial imposters found their way on stage! Men and women, who by way of deceit, tell fraudulent life stories to upset the theatre-goers!

When the audience realizes a betrayal, collective groans and scattered whimpers are painfully heard over the general dismay. Empaths intensely dislike these inauthentic moments, while phonies love seeing the audience be tricked! They are fraudsters who lie for the vicarious thrill of deception! Theatre Junkies!

Fortunately, a recent change of EE policy has been successful in reducing the number of acting out imposters.

CHAPTER 6

When Jordana left the stage that night, she was invited to join Mrs. Ubergang and her husband. It was quite a thrill meeting the founder of the Empathic Movement. The three of them chatted as the Theatre prepared for the next to share. While waiting, Jordana witnessed a ticketing by the EE, sending a shiver up her spine.

At first, she wrote it off as a delayed reaction to her Theatre experience. But her mind continued to circle with curiosity concerning the inner workings of the Theatre.

Jordana was not the first to wonder. But such musings were usually brief before fading into the soothing calm of the community. An extensive air of serenity lulled concerns that crossed people's minds. However, Jordana's transformation only minutes before emboldened an inquiry. Mr. Ubergang readily responded with a general overview, as Mrs. Ubergang became quiet. Because the leader of the Empathic Movement has never been keen on "enforcing empathy," she left the EE to her husband and assumed a position of *blind faith*. The general public in turn was wholeheartedly behind the EE and their devotion to the Empathic Movement.

Jordana thought more about the Theatre, until a wave of delightfulness flowed, immersing her in an awe induced acceptance.

Soon after, the three of them politely parted. Mr. Ubergang watched Jordana slowly meander from the Theatre, just to insure her absence.

Loyal and protective to a fault, Mr. Ubergang has been strongly motivated to insure his wife's continued success.

As the Director of EE, he believes in the logicality of policy and the importance to take care of repeat offenders smoothly and efficiently. Mr. Ubergang fully accepts that his mission is to maintain a peaceful community.

Those who stood out time and time again as not being a part of the tranquility were prevailed upon to never cause emotional pain again. So on the day of that night's new moon, the EE prepared to carry out their duty. Second hands completed circles in unison, as the sun crossed the sky in its constant and faithful manner. Then the night fell, with exacting precision.

The End

Sci Fi Psy

CHAPTER 1

Miss Sheltermann-

Hi, How are you?

B. Arnold-

Not good. First I want to apologize for being late. I was with friends planning stuff. I would've called, but my cell was dead.

Miss Sheltermann-

I understand. How's your recovery? That was quite a fall you took.

B. Arnold-

I'm okay. I was in the hospital for weeks, now I'm better. That's when I got to know Jack. He's why I'm here. But first I need to ask. Do you know I was seeing Eleanor Phytt? I guess so, if you know of my fall. I was seeing her weekly but she no longer wants to work with me.

Miss Sheltermann-

Yes, I do know. What happened with seeing her?

B. Arnold-

I'm not certain. I know I was kinda stuck and couldn't figure out what to do. But isn't that why people go to therapy?

Miss Sheltermann-

Yes, that's true.

B. Arnold-

I liked Ms. Phytt, but she said that maybe somebody else could help me better.

Miss Sheltermann-

How do you feel about changing therapists?

B. Arnold-

It's my fault. She just didn't like me, or something. I don't know. I think I had trouble trusting her. Well, maybe it's for the best. I hope I can trust you.

Miss Sheltermann-

I hope that you can. I am here to help you, whatever your concern is.

B. Arnold-

I'm glad to hear th**at**.

Miss Sheltermann-

Oh, I'm sorry, I haven't introduced myself. I am Michelle Sheltermann. Do you wish for me to call you Miss Arnold?

B. Arnold-

No, you can call me B.

Miss Sheltermann-

As you wish. So B, I am generally familiar with why you're here, but perhaps you can tell me in your own words why you've decided to be in therapy?

B. Arnold-

The reason I've come here is because, well, I am in a relationship with Jack and I love him. He wants to marry me.

Miss Sheltermann-

So help me understand what your concern is, as that sounds like it could be a good thing.

B. Arnold-

It does feel good, but I am not sure that it's fair that I marry him.

Miss Sheltermann-

Why wouldn't it be fair?

B. Arnold-

Well, I've got certain qualities that I don't like. I'm afraid they will hurt him.

Miss Sheltermann-

Tell me what you mean?

B. Arnold-

I can't. As Miss Phytt said, I have a secret.

Miss Sheltermann-

A secret? Does Jack know of your secret?

B. Arnold-

No, but it's not about him knowing, it's that if I marry him, I may harm him...I feel so ashamed.

Miss Sheltermann-

Does your shame keep you from talking more of your secret?

B. Arnold-

Of course it does. I couldn't live with myself if I hurt Jack.

Miss Sheltermann-

If you were to hurt Jack.

B. Arnold-

Yes, but I don't want to hurt him. I met him two years ago. He and I work at the Apple store. I didn't really know him until my accident. That's when he came to visit me in the hospital. Jack is the sweetest guy you'll ever meet. I've never met anyone so nice. The folks that live here are just so goodhearted. Where I'm from it's much more competitive and my kind are just not nice.

Miss Sheltermann-

Your kind?

B. Arnold-

Well, what I mean is, those who live where I'm from don't show they care like people around here do.

Miss Sheltermann-

You were talking about Jack, now you're talking about two geographical areas. Help me understand.

B. Arnold-

You're right, I was and I am.

Miss Sheltermann-

Sorry?

B. Arnold-

I did mean this area, with Jack in particular.

Miss Sheltermann-

Oh, ok.

B. Arnold-

So what do I do?

Miss Sheltermann-

About what?

B. Arnold-

Should I marry him? He wants children.

Miss Sheltermann-

Do you?

B. Arnold-

Yes, but I 'm afraid of what will follow.

Miss Sheltermann -

What do you mean?

B. Arnold-

He could die.

Miss Sheltermann-

Who could die? Jack could die? Why do you say this?

B. Arnold-

I just know it.

Miss Sheltermann-

Is this part of your secret?

B. Arnold-

I can't tell you anything more!

Miss Sheltermann-

B, with all due respect, this is what you talked about with your previous therapist.

After 9 sessions you were still unable to tell her what you were referring to. What would it be like if you shared your secret with me?

B. Arnold-

I cannot, that would be a betrayal.

Miss Sheltermann-

To Jack? To yourself? To someone else?

SILENCE.

Miss Sheltermann-

Do you feel at risk to harm Jack or yourself?

B. Arnold-

No, believe me I would tell you if I felt that way.

Miss Sheltermann-

Ok. But please call me at any time should you need to. We have to end for today. Are you okay?

B. Arnold-

Yeah, I'm all right for now.

Miss Sheltermann-

Will you come in next week to talk more?

B. Arnold-

Yes, I must.

Miss Sheltermann-

I can see you Thursday at 11.

B. Arnold-

That's good. I'll make sure to be on time.

CHAPTER 2

It was quite evident that something was very, very, odd. Isolated reports trickled from a triangle of towns in New Hampshire of people somehow surviving lethal situations. Fantastic stories of falls from great heights, brutal car collisions and other head-scratching happenings were recounted. **The**se inexplicable occurrences captured the public's curiosity and apprehension. Many people, both survivors of these events and witnesses to them were referred for psychological treatment. Due to the catchment area, one mental health clinic had a front row seat to these phenomena by treating patients related to these strange events.

Healthcare companies had a spate of PTSD fill their diagnostic slots as Incident Debriefing workshops were put into action. Many folks filled the chairs looking to explain the unexplainable. Some turned to the idea of divine intervention to make sense of it all, while other explanations reverberated, rippling randomly to the community at large.

Meanwhile, clinicians forged ahead, working ardently to help patients cope with their trauma. Some therapists performed EMDR, others used more traditional methods.

Due to the spectacular nature of the presenting problem, curiosity generated much discussion among the clinical staff.

Concern over HIPAA laws was carefully attended to, as cases were conferenced within legal guidelines.

Over time, bewilderment ballooned, as psychotherapists were stymied trying to make sense of it all. Although witnesses to the events faded from treatment, almost all of those who survived their lethal situation continued. The staff wondered, "How could these people have survived such serious injuries?"

Although patients were willing to talk of their trauma, a number of therapists intuited that their patients were withholding something important. They couldn't explain why, only that it was their gut instinct. At treatment conference later that week, Miss Sheltermann strengthened the idea by reporting her patient's reference to having a secret. That formed a general consensus that some concealed element appeared to be paramount to a larger picture.

Therapists explored and delved, looking for the nexus. Out of a compelling inquisitiveness, they compared other aspects reported by these trauma-surviving patients. Co-existing symptoms began to line up with confusing regularity.

Difficulties with relationships, particularly sexual dysfunction, had an unusually high rate of co-incidence, occurring *before* the reported traumatic event. Clinicians were baffled. "What commonality could these two factors have?"

Tracking cause and effect to understand how events relate routinely presses upon therapists. Hence, it was no surprise that a dogged pursuit took hold as clinicians faced this riddle. Yet, they did not lose focus, and continued to work for the benefit of all their patients.

CHAPTER 3

Konn Jimm was overseeing a limited pilot program. The detachment was one of scores implemented across a large targeted area testing the feasibility of a full frontal attack. Forces landed at a number of locations, as broad and scattered as the stars in the sky. Konn Jimm's assignment was considered less desirable than others. But, he was in no position to buck it, as politics and his past had decided the path. Nonetheless, here in enemy territory Konn Jimm held on, as his soldiers stepped off to carry out their mission.

CHAPTER 4

In her lifetime, Mischen knew nothing of war. As the Clinical Director of the mental health clinic, "Caring Folks, Here to Help," she helped change thousands of lives for the better. A kind woman of gentle roots, Mischen was a scholar and a mensch, a seasoned veteran with 40 years of experience as a psychotherapist. But despite Mischen's easygoing demeanor, she could be quite determined to adapt and master the reality at hand.

Both of Mischen's parents were Holocaust survivors. That fact had a significant impact upon her life. She always made it her business to arm herself with the weaponry of an empathic connection. Empathy lent clarity and direction in the most difficult clinical situations.

On this particular Sunday in October, Mischen was alone, sitting quietly in her office. As the sun streamed in at a late afternoon slant, she felt considerably in the dark. A faraway and fixed gaze followed another particularly baffling session.

She felt no closer to understanding these patients, nor the cluster of events that precipitated their therapy. Yet, she firmly believed in the existence of a unifying factor that would explain the patients' symptoms, intra-psychic dynamics and inconceivable survival.

Mischen sat transfixed as the afternoon waned. As the sun began to halve on the horizon the room darkened. Suddenly, a bright light of urgency overcame her. A deep unsettling feeling filled her being. Inexplicable and compelling, her momentary contemplation swung into immediate action. Reaching for her Apple device, she sent a text, requiring all clinicians to clear their schedule for an important meeting, *Tuesday Afternoon.*

CHAPTER 5

Tuesday came slowly leading Mischen to arrive early.

Although appearing her usual self, a quiet intensity was evident. As staff began to stream into the conference room, she took a sober look at each of them. Since most of them had worked at the clinic for many years, Mischen knew their families and imagined their faces as well.

The 11 and their many were alive within her as she prepared for a pivotal meeting. Although a number of staff had to change a commitment at home or the office, there was no grumbling or grousing, as Mischen was respected without reservation. The unusual nature of this puzzling issue cemented the staff's full attention.

Mischen spoke, "We all know why we're here. We've been treating a select population of patients who share curious issues for some time now. Despite our best efforts we have been unsuccessfully empathic to them as individuals or as a group. Clearly we're missing something. I am growing quite concerned, as my curiosity has morphed into feeling unnerved." At that, the group began to shift uncomfortably in their seats.

"We must use our clinical skills to understand this phenomena.

It is my belief there is one common factor unifying all these cases. But before we open the floor, let me share with you a specific protocol I am requesting we follow. This may seem odd or uncalled for, but until this conundrum is resolved, I would like us to address each other formally by our surname. Don't ask how this will assist, it's purely intuitive on my part. Since I have the responsibility of this operation, I will be the only exception and will continue to be addressed by my first name. Please take a moment and let each of us know your preferred prefix."

The group naturally responded in a clockwise direction.

"Mr. Stryker." "Mrs. Morter." "Ms. Rampart." "Dr. Winchester." "Miss Phytt." "Mr. Archer." "Dr. Duggin." "Miss Sheltermann." "Ms. D'Fents." "Mrs. Wynne." "Miss Peace."

"Thank you." Mischen said.

"One other issue before proceeding. I want to highlight the importance of absolute confidentiality. I know all of you have a high regard for patients' rights. However, we are human and may be tempted to tell a loved one details of this perplexing situation. But we cannot. It is paramount that we maintain complete secrecy.

From this moment forward, I would like to refer to us as 'The Circle Few.' The few, who are dedicated to know what there *is* to know. We *will* discover their secret! By way of empathy we will arrive at the focal point where commonalities converge. Let us be free with our imagination."

With that in mind, Mischen asked of the Few, "What are the facts? What do we know for certain? What is conjecture?"

As staff spoke, Miss Phytt wrote on a white board, allowing the specifics to resonate.

What is known

They have survived events ordinarily lethal. Many appear to be harboring a secret. Almost all have relationship difficulties. Many report sexual dysfunction that pre-existed their traumatic incident. Several state that they have relocated from the Pacific Northwest. Their choice of words is occasionally odd and they appear to have an indiscernible accent. Many have feelings of resentment toward authority. Some act inconsiderately toward clinicians.

Unconscious themes

A number of clinical hypotheses were entertained as an informal discussion burgeoned. Although the group worked through cross talk years ago, this provocative clinical conundrum had a regressive impact. Mischen had to remind staff to not verbally step on one another. Copious notes were taken as the meeting progressed.

Patient themes included: Inner conflict. Withholding. Untrusting. Excessive guilt. Persecutory fantasies. Grandiosity. Fear of being found out. Missing their home.

Mischen then decided to hone in. "Let's look at the particulars and draw a larger picture. Why would these patients be feeling these feelings? And how do near death experiences relate to their therapy? Why would the confluence of sexual and intimacy problems exist before the incidents occurred? Why is the superego such a factor here? What is their inner conflict?"

Although the Few responded to these questions nothing insightful was born.

Mischen broke a contemplative silence, "Let's go back to the presenting problem. They survive impossible odds, withhold a secret, and don't trust us. Perhaps coming close to their physical demise has left them cautious and wary of others? Yet, our work with them has been nothing but supportive and caring."

Mischen hesitated as she looked out the window at the trees and sky. "Why would they not trust *us*? Are they exercising projection in some way? Is the threat really from *them*?"

Silence.

"Let's stay with that for a moment," she said.

"It sounds like some sort of Sci-Fi movie," Mrs. Morter said.

Dr. Winchester reacted quickly, "This is serious, let's try not to..." Mischen interrupted him, "No, go with that. Does anyone have a similar association?"

"Yes," Ms. D'Fents said, "It reminds me of the 1956 movie, "Invasion of the Body Snatchers.""

"Tell us." Mischen said with an edge to her tone.

"Oh, that's the movie where Aliens from outer space come to earth and take the form of humans..."

An audible gasp punctured the room, followed by dead silence. Ms. Rampart nervously laughed, then lowered her head.

Furtive looks circulated the room, bringing the wordless moment to its knees. The notion seemed so fantastic that no one could even whisper the words. The door of reason knocked hard of other. Then, suddenly, several blurted out, "Maybe they're not real people! Maybe they're from outer space!" A cacophony of cross talk vaulted to air, as steadfast denial pulsated with fear.

Mischen waited before stepping in. "We must consider this idea, as preposterous as it may sound..."

Dr. Winchester interrupted, "This is crazy!"

Mischen emphasized with a firm but measured tone, "We cannot stand idly by. We must identify what is real and what is not."

CHAPTER 6

As mentioned, Konn Jimm is commander for one of the scores of operations implanted in star systems across the Milky Way galaxy. Receiving his assignment to invade Earth, prompted ridicule from his peers, as it was too far and "400 earth years" too late. They claimed the local earthlings had already plundered the planet of its beauty, resources, and life forms.

Even though Konn Jimm's soldiers were schooled in being amiable and affable, the general disposition of the Aliens was often arrogant and unfeeling. Although this made it easier to carry out the incursion, many were conflicted about their presence in a foreign land.

Almost all of the Aliens drafted during peacetime felt betrayed, as the earthly words, *meet the new boss, same as the old boss,* were applicable to their foreign experience.

Soon after attaining power and despite promises to the contrary, the new leader changed his policy to an ambitious plan of conquering countless life forms across an expanse of light-years.

Yes, this assignment had its adventure and excitement, but for many it brought resentment and resignation as it took them from their lives at home.

Konn Jimm felt similarly. Like many soldiers he wished to be at home, living in peace. But this venture had to do with rites of passage and his being seen as a "Man" among his kind.

The soldiers, who were all of childbearing age, learned our earthly rituals and languages, while existing in entirely different bodies. At first, most found the experience unique and pleasing, but negotiating a new body was encumbering, as the clumsiness of their carry gave them away at 100 yards. Early on bumping into things was a constant, which led to a series of embarrassing apologies. Hardly the image of an average soldier at the front, but the front it was.

For some, sensation, movement and choice proved to be an enticing invitation.

Intoxicated by the many engaging applications of the human body, some strayed from their mission by getting entangled with substance and or the law.

Others attracted public attention by way of reckless behavior. Some survivors of "lethal situations" were experimenting with their earth-bound limits. Konn Jimm recognized that this brought unwelcome media coverage, which could threaten their mission, so he stepped in, to contain the acting out.

CHAPTER 7

Once the incredulous idea of an Alien invasion was said out loud, a dam of denial burst. A wild flurry of ideas flowed from the Few, as one possibility was swiftly replaced with another. Seemingly unrelated symptoms were now connected, as action and reaction drew lines of causation. A wealth of clinical material coalesced into workable assumptions. Therapists did what they do best, imagining freely to facilitate empathy. All the while, Mischen let the process unfold, as she had done with patients for decades.

The Few knew that constructing reality by cobbling together reports of Aliens from outer space has its cautionary caveats. They were quite mindful that no longer being restricted to earth-bound laws of cause and effect has its interpretive risks.

As minds and mouths began to slow, all thought the wall clock ran way fast. As the staff looked to leave, Mischen emphasized, "Like any running hypothesis, it is important to seek confirmation. We must know the truth! Lives are at stake. The welfare of all mankind may be in abeyance. There can be no wavering. We cannot dither. However, we must maintain our sense of balance. We must be vigorous, yet exercise objective restraint. Both will serve us well. Let us move forward without fear. I have full confidence that we will be successful."

The staff was stunned as they filed from the room. In all the days and decades of their professional practice, they had never dealt with a more insane sounding notion.

CHAPTER 8

One week later, Miss Sheltermann arrived for case conference after a session with an "alleged Alien" just minutes before. She could barely contain herself as the staff filled the room. With a nod, Mischen yielded the floor. Miss Sheltermann felt strangely self-conscious being the purveyor of such immense news.

"There's been a major breakthrough," she said, with a combination of excitement and dread. "They *are* Aliens! My patient B Arnold just told me. Their mission is to take over our towns, our cities, then the whole world!"

Suddenly, Miss Sheltermann became woozy and had to sit down. Mr. Stryker eased her into a chair. The room darkened, as the sun hid behind the clouds. Blocks away, a dog could be heard barking plaintively. The staff was in shock. No one could speak.

Long moments passed before Mischen asked, "What else do you know?"

Catching her breath, Miss Sheltermann said, "The Aliens are here from another world to, as my patient said, 'propagate' with humans. They plan on creating native Alien offspring by breeding with humans. The product will look human, but in reality they'll be Aliens! In addition, the human parent will die within several years. The Invaders will gain in numbers and eventually dominate the world!"

A burst of words surged, as Mischen contained hers. Staff quickly quieted as Miss Sheltermann continued, "The Aliens are easily identifiable. The pinky on their left hand is longer than their ring finger." Several staff members excitedly agreed that they too noticed that aberration.

Suddenly, Miss Peace's eyes flew wide as she interrupted, "I know why there's so much sexual dysfunction with the Aliens! They have difficulty performing because consummating their relationship sentences their human 'lover' to death!"

Mischen and the Few marveled at Miss Peace's imaginative and viable idea.

But Miss Sheltermann's expression brought them back to her disturbing report. "I can't believe," she moaned, "what else my patient said." Staff froze in their seats. Miss Sheltermann looked at the floor before throwing her head back blurting out, "B says that the Aliens are immortal." A guttural sound was heard, as the spirit in the room was rendered faint and feeble. Mischen closed her eyes slowly and took a deep deliberate breath.

No one could have anticipated the final weight about to crush down upon them. Miss Sheltermann continued, "But there is one exception, one way they can be stopped. They perish if they self-destruct…if they commit suicide."

An immediate body blow of emotions overpowered them all. Fear and confusion cast their net, immobilizing the moment. Some directly realized the implications, while others did not. One by one by another, Mischen saw in each face the moment of awareness that cast light upon the darkness of their inherited duty. Mr. Stryker, a Vietnam veteran did the math quickly saying quietly to no one in particular, "I can't believe this, so many years since death was all around me. Now it comes again." He shook his head, "We didn't sign up for this."

Mischen stepped in as the voice of reason.

"We must have courage and be prepared to act. Although much is unknown we must move forward confirming evidence and preparing a plan. We can wish all we want that this invasion is just someone's paranoid delusion, but that would be ignoring strong signs to the contrary.

It appears that we've been thrust into an unimaginable reality. Surreal as it may feel, we must seriously consider Aliens are real and pose an immediate threat to us all."

The staff sat staring at Mischen as they listened to her every word.

"Will we lead the enemy to their demise? Can we access a primitive part of ourselves to insure we'll survive? Will we feel empowered to respond to this tectonic shift of responsibility? If we know that certain actions are necessary, will our inner tools be available? As clinical soldiers, we need to be unrelentingly objective. We must clearly be cognizant of counter-transferential minefields emerging from the reversal of our clinical directive."

No one took a breath or blinked as Mischen continued. "We have always worked diligently to help, to rescue others from pain and suffering. Now it appears we are called upon to exercise the opposite. Yet, if this is the reality we face, we'll still be rescuing those in need, only on a grander scale, as our catchment area numbers will balloon to 7 billion people. Meanwhile, our fellow humans may be unaware of this existential threat. We may be the first line of defense to the Invasion. If that's so, then we are present day Minute Men of our Revolutionary days past..."

Mischen paused, as her determination hardened. "From this moment on, we commit our all, fully awake to this historical happening. These fiends are heinous Invaders, moving into our neighborhood with their smiling faces and evil thoughts, breathing and scheming in the house across the street... Although it remains unclear how we will proceed, proceed we must!"

"Let us meet tomorrow."

CHAPTER 9

Mischen met the next day with turncoat B Arnold.

"Thank you for coming in," Mischen said upon greeting her. "Considering what you revealed to Miss Sheltermann, it's important for us to talk. I should tell you that due to Federal Laws of Confidentiality I cannot reveal the identity of anyone who attends here or anything about them. But those same laws do not prohibit you from telling me about them."

B responded, "I understand."

"What should you tell me?" Mischen asked.

B felt good sharing, "I want to tell you that the life of everyone on this planet is in jeopardy. Miss Sheltermann told you, yes?"

"Yes, but please tell me in your own words," Mischen said.

As the Alien spoke, Mischen assessed the veracity of her claims by emotional attunement and attention to detail. She sensed B to be both consistent and genuine. When B finished, she appeared relieved, yet vulnerable, not knowing what to expect from Mischen.

Mischen asked, "What do you expect me to do with this information?"

B replied, "It's not what *I* expect, it's what *you* feel is right to do. I no longer have a hidden agenda. There is one thing though that is unacceptable to me."

Mischen coolly asked, "What are you referring to?"

B leaned forward and said, "Under no circumstances do you contact the FBI or any other law enforcement. That would complicate your efforts. I also don't want to end up being mentally or physically tortured."

Mischen looked her in the eyes and said, "That's not the kind of country we have."

With an edge in her voice B responded, "Please, don't—how do you say—adult my intelligence? I have studied the history of your world and know of fairly recent international events. I do not wish to find myself in a similar situation."

Mischen lost whatever neutral tone she had. "You make that statement, yet, you are a part of an Invasion putting the lives of billions in peril."

"Yes, that's true. But I am here telling you of this danger, aren't I?"

Mischen softened, "Yes, we're very thankful for that."

"If you do contact the authorities, I'll deny everything and stonewall the process. Your other patients will end up being hurt the most in that situation."

Mischen closed her eyes as she bowed her head in agreement, "OK." B appeared empowered as she made her final request, "I also want complete immunity in whatever develops."

Mischen answered firmly, "That I can't promise, but I will advocate for you."

Seconds ticked before Mischen added, "So, how can I be convinced you're telling the truth? How can I know for sure who is involved? This is a matter of utmost importance. I don't want to take action based upon one person's report."

B confidently replied, "I can tell you the names of those involved. I can speak my native language for you right now."

"That's fine," Mischen said, "but I want irrefutable proof."

"How can I provide that?" queried B.

Mischen felt a disturbingly powerful feeling as she replied, "I'd like a sample of your DNA."

"I have no problem with that."

"Today."

"Ok."

"Right now."

"All right."

Mischen was prepared with a doctor, the technology and the proper papers to protect the clinic ethically and legally. In a matter of minutes a sample was taken and sent for processing. The fact that Mischen's sister-in-law was a molecular biologist promised a quick turnaround. Mischen knew she could trust her.

CHAPTER 10

That next morning prior to the clinical meeting, Dr. Winchester had an early session with an alleged Alien.

Dr. Winchester-

Hello Nik.

Nik-

Hi Doc.

Dr. Winchester-

How are you?

Nik-

I'm fine. Really, I'm fine.

Dr. Winchester-

Why the *really, I'm fine*? You said it as if you were trying to convince me.

Nik-

What do you mean I was trying to convince you? I was just answering your question! I don't get your psycho mumbo jumbo. Always judging me! What a bunch of cow crap!

Silence.

Dr. Winchester-

Do you want to tell me more about your feelings?

Nik-

Why, so you can see me ticked off? Are you *trying* to make me angry?

Dr. Winchester-

Why would I want to do that?

Nik-

I don't know, you tell me! You've been picking at me for weeks.

Dr. Winchester-

In what way?

Nik-

You know what way. I come here 'cause I can't have a hard time with my girlfriend. It still doesn't work! You haven't helped me one bit. I should just quit.

Dr. Winchester-

What are your thoughts about that Nik?

Nik-

Oh, back on me again!

Dr. Winchester-

Didn't you say last week that therapy helps you blow off steam?

Nik-

I must've been crazy to say that. Hey! Why are you staring at my hand? You keep looking at it. What's your problem? Huh?

Dr. Winchester-

I'm sorry. I didn't mean to make you feel self-conscious. However, I've noticed that your left hand is different than your right. How is that for you?

Nik-

It's fine! What difference does it make?...How 'bout answering me!

Dr. Winchester-

You seem worked up this morning. Did something just happen? Are you under the influence of something?

Nik-

No, I'm not! But explain to me why my hand is so important!

Dr. Winchester-

Sometimes if someone feels inadequate, it can transpose to a physical symptom like impotency.

Nik-

Impotency, inadequacy, gee Doc, you sure can be supportive! You Doctor, are a jerk! And what's your American saying? What goes around comes around back?

Dr. Winchester-

Are you threatening me? I am not comfortable with this Nik. I think it's best that we end for today.

Nik-

Fine! Mark my words though. You and your world are on the way out! Everyone in this clinic, in this country, will be toast. *We will bury you!*

Dr. Winchester-

Are you serious about hurting people?

Nik-

No!

Nik barked as he slammed the door behind him.

CHAPTER 11

Mischen arrived early, anticipating the lab result. Dr. Winchester's face brightened when he saw she was in.

"Mischen, are you free?" Dr. Winchester queried. "Yes."

Dr. Winchester recounted what Nik had said, but Mischen said nothing. Dr. Winchester thought it odd, but trusted his Director and gravitated to the window, watching other staff enter the building.

Soon after her second cup of coffee, the phone rang. Mischen showed no expression as she was told the DNA test results.

At first, Mischen did not appear any different than other mornings. But soon it was noticeable that her eyes were watching an internal movie. She busied herself preparing the chairs and re-positioning her coffee cup. The Circle Few sat down in their usual seats.

"Ladies and gentlemen, the news is not good. It is confirmed beyond a doubt, that they are Aliens." Eyes opened wide as jaws dropped. She continued, "They intend on killing us all, over time.

Although Dr. Winchester's patient validated our hypothesis, the turncoat's DNA test was indisputable. The molecular biologist said, quote, 'I can say with absolute certainty, it is not human.' She went on to say that it is completely different than any DNA on Earth, period."

Swallowing hard she took a few moments to collect herself. All eyes were on her as staff sat immobile. No words could express the primeval expression on their faces. Although crises of survival have been ordinary for humans throughout all of time, it was rare in the present day lives of the Few.

Suddenly Miss Phytt blurted out, "We have to call the Police and the FBI!"

Miss Peace responded directly, "Stop! Think for a moment. Imagine if we did contact the authorities, this clinic would be awash with FBI agents. As potential suspects, every patient would have their file analyzed and be subject to interrogation. There would be no consideration for privacy or confidentiality. Consider being swarmed by a gaggle of G-men, who, over time, could induce PTSD en masse. We also can't rule out a possible wave of vigilantism, where anyone suspected of being in therapy could be attacked. It seems to me that first and foremost, we have a responsibility to protect our present non-Alien patients, as well as the people in our community. We need to keep our heads and act in a deliberate manner. If not, we could miss an opportunity and fall under the oppression of the Invasion."

Silence.

"Yet, we cannot underestimate these Invaders." Mischen firmly added, "They have traveled far and have immense powers, evidenced by their ability to assume our physical bodies. We must convince them in no uncertain terms that the Earth is not theirs to take, it is ours to keep. We love our home. Innumerable times in history courageous men and women have fought against tyranny. Untold numbers have sacrificed their lives to save mankind from maniacal ambition.

Now we face a crossroads. Will we prevail or will mankind be doomed? We must embrace the side of us that will do battle. We must not retreat or doubt our purpose. We must stand for those who stood for us, as we stand for those yet to come. With love in our hearts for all mankind, we *will* defeat them. We *will* drive them out!

Let us break here and retire to our offices. I would like everyone to feel and reflect upon this extraordinary situation. In addition, I ask for your specific ideas on initiating a plan of action. We will meet at 11. Let this be '*Our Finest Hour*.'"

CHAPTER 12

An hour later staff walked in as if carrying hundred pound sacks on their backs. The reality of the Invasion was a burden that weighed heavily, submerging their faith and hope.

Mischen began. "Before we open the floor, I want to acknowledge the extraordinary situation that we face. It is a tremendous weight for all of us to bear. However, if it had to happen, better for it to happen here. The world is fortunate to have this fall upon us. I have full confidence that we will be successful. We *will be* proud. Now, what do you have for our cause?"

"Yes, Mr. Archer."

"In anticipation of this meeting I have printed off a map through Google pinpointing the radius of these mysterious survivals. A perimeter has been established. As you can see the..."

As he opened the map, staff shifted to his side. Had the room been a boat, it would have capsized. But the Few were quite steady on their feet, instinctively buoyed by a male leader. The initial loss of wind in their sails was reversed, as Mr. Archer's input lifted the heavy anchors of failure and doubt. The Few felt solid again as they began to navigate on a course of courage and purpose.

"Where are you going with this?" Mischen asked.

Mr. Archer replied, "I feel it's important to take a proactive position. I'm recommending we identify the specific location of our targeted population."

Dr. Winchester hastily jumped in, "How can we do that? We can't anticipate where they're going to show up."

"Yes, that's true but we can extend past the known area and ..." "And do what Mr. Archer?" Dr. Winchester said impatiently.

Maintaining his balance, Mr. Archer said, "We can capitalize on the weakness of the ghouls by sketching a preliminary fortification. I propose an immediate series of workshops spreading past the occupied perimeter of the enemy. It is my plan to hold 6 to 8 workshops within the targeted area within 3 to 4 weeks." "Workshops?" several staff chimed.

"Yes, workshops. We will have a major thrust of clinical education around the prevention of suicide."

"Prevention? How would that help us?" Ms. Morter asked, as her eyebrows knitted to one.

Mr. Archer proceeded without hesitation, "These workshops will detail preventing suicide. And in doing so, we'll highlight factors that *can* lead to suicide, thus educating clinicians in advance of the possible need. The troops will be prepared for battle should the perimeter be broken. In the interim, we will do a service for clinicians throughout the area."

Mischen responded, "That is a very wise plan. Let's proceed directly. I'll secure strategic locations. Who will assist Mr. Archer with the curriculum and the workshops? Yes, Dr. Winchester. Ms. Rampart. Thank you."

Mischen continued, "What else? Yes, Mrs. Morter. What would you like to say?"

"In the interest of leading the Aliens to their demise, it may be helpful if we put a face on the enemy."

"Tell us what you mean." Mischen asked.

"Right now, the enemy is indiscernible from our neighbors. In fact, they may be our neighbors."

Suddenly, Mrs. Wynne burst into tears. Mischen followed the groups lead and chose not to stop and inquire. She made a mental note to talk with her later.

"So how would you put a face on them?" inquired Mischen.

Mrs. Morter shared her idea, "Well, what if the turncoat was willing to describe what they really look like? I'm sure they look a lot different than we do."

Mischen cocked her head, "Miss Phytt, you can draw, would you be willing to work with her?"

With a wavering voice, Miss Phytt said, "Ah, yes, sure. I haven't drawn in a while, but I'll do my best."

Miss Sheltermann inserted, "I think it's a great idea. B tells me they're about 5 feet tall and look like insects. Yeah, let's see them as they really are, vile and revolting murderers, heartlessly wanting to rob us of our progeny."

Secretly, Mischen was pleased to hear the inflammatory words. She knew stirring up the "smell of blood" would allow for primitive instincts to surface. For decades, the staff had tailored care and concern for others, but now needed access to their primal selves to defend and protect their fellow man.

Mr. Stryker spoke next, "I will be leading a group for all staff on Thursday mornings focusing on, well, there's no other way to say it, killing the enemy or being killed yourself. Through eons of time, it has sadly been the primary dichotomy of all human beings."

Mischen nodded in approval.

"I have to be honest," Julia Rampart suddenly said. "This enabling of someone's suicide is not for me. I like people." All eyes shifted to Mischen, who waited for Ms. Rampart to finish.

"Ms. Rampart, no one likes this idea in the least. I know there isn't a warmonger among you. But we must recognize the reality we face. These monsters have come from outer space to kill us. Our caring hearts for those in need must now turn stone cold.

Our minds, employed to understand, must be calculating and deceiving. Our hands, which have lifted so many, must tighten around their necks. We must outsmart the evil that seeks our demise. We shall use the smiling faces of our loved ones to inspire our march to blot the Aliens out.

Each Alien death is *our children's, children's, children's* assurance of life. As students we took a pledge of allegiance to America. Now we must broaden our allegiance to include all mankind. We have no other choice. We must face the demands that confront us. But we must never act alone. The decision to terminate must be unanimous. All 12 of us decide, case by case."

Silence descended, then Mischen added, "Let us not forget the commitment to our other patients. We must continue our fine work. It will be challenging as we shift from helping patients, to exacting the opposite with Alien patients."

CHAPTER 13

It was midday and the leader of the incursion was just rolling out of bed. Konn Jimm seemed quite content with the present status of the Invasion. After all, the structure was in place. He insured that his soldiers had lodging, employment and no shortage of potential partners to fulfill their mission. Still, Konn could not come to odds with war being waged by way of amorous advances in the field. But he was getting used to it, assisted by a woman named Sarita.

His soldiers were at best conflicted about their mission. Their feelings affected their behavior in various ways, accounting for their involvement in psychotherapy. But despite their mixed feelings, the existential threat to the human race was no less real. Although "Caring Folks, Here To Help" was unaware of the exact number of Aliens mobilized, the Circle Few proceeded ahead, quite aware that the outcome of this offensive could impact the whole world.

CHAPTER 14

Aliens were not the only ones who were conflicted. Miss Phytt spoke in supervision.

"Thanks so much for squeezing me in today, Ms. D'Fents."

"You're welcome Miss Phytt." They smiled at the formality.

"I didn't want to wait till Thursday. I have to say, I am having a very difficult time."

"Tell me."

Miss Phytt sighed, quickly feeling soothed in the company of her supervisor.

"You know me. You know my work. It's no secret that I grew up in an alcoholic home. You know that I can over-identify and try too hard to rescue folks. But you also know of my own therapy and that I'm a good clinician."

"Of course you are Eleanor, everyone knows that."

Miss Phytt added, "But despite all that, I have great difficulty carrying out our new objective."

"You're not alone," Ms. D'Fents said with a reassuring tone.

"We're all struggling with it."

She paused before adding, "It is so curious. At the heart of our work over the years has been compassion. But now, that same feeling complicates our task with the Aliens. Feeling sorry for them only makes it more difficult. What was a natural ally in treatment is now a powerful liability.

Yet on the other hand, empathy remains invaluable in treating human or Alien. Knowing the internal experience of another, equips us to be successful agents of change. It is so strange."

Miss Phytt shook her head in agreement. "I have 4 Aliens. When they talk about their pain and conflict, I identify with them. Knowing their evil intent only mollifies my compassion for a few minutes. It is so natural to again feel *their* pain! I think it'd be different had we known they were Aliens from the beginning of treatment, rather than after months of connecting with them."

"I see your point," said Ms. D'Fents. "It *is* very challenging. I've got 3 of 'em. I work very hard to be in tune with what they're saying while not losing awareness of their genocidal intent. Twice recently my feelings got blurred between our mission and theirs. That's not good. I must stay the path and not stray from the way. The more sessions, the more I feel their underlying motives. Our work is disturbing, but necessary. Michelle, I mean, Miss Sheltermann, presently works with three Aliens who talk openly about the Invasion. My patients have yet to progress to that level."

"Twice, I've had Aliens come close to revealing and then back off," Miss Phytt reported weakly. "The whole thing is just unbelievable," she said shaking her head.

Ms. D'Fents replied, "It really is. It's so hard to imagine that it's real, but it is. We need to stick together. We have a job to do."

"Yes we do. Thanks Martha," Miss Phytt said feeling fortified.

"See you Thursday," they said in unison.

"Oh, I meant to ask you, have you seen this?"

Ms. D'Fents fumbled with a sliding high-pile stack of papers shifting across her desk. "I know, I know, I need to catch up on filing," she expressed rotely. "Ah, here it is, I knew it was here. Check this out." "Wow, they knocked it out quickly." Miss Phytt said, as she scanned the flyer. "I'll check it out later after my patient. Thanks."

Considerations of Suicide

Not identifying, nor resolving a patient's internal conflicts can lead them to gravitate toward suicide as a relief from their feelings.

If a clinician fails to make a timely referral for medication, it may increase the chances that the person could fall prey to their own hand.

If the therapist does not consistently convey to patients a feeling of being understood, they are more likely to doubt themselves, feel alone and lose hope in their heart.

A therapist who does not keep their word to the patient about fees, appointment times, etc., can confuse and disrupt the patient's equilibrium. This can lessen one's belief in the process of therapy and could ultimately lead to a serious emotional downslide.

A patient struggling with emotional instability is more apt to act on impulse if the means (e.g. a gun) is easily available.

If a clinician overlooks - for whatever reason - the subtle start or evidence of self-destructive feelings, it raises the risk that a momentum gathering inertia could lead to an impulsive act.

Arguing with a patient or giving an ultimatum when she/he is under the influence or emotionally unstable, puts the patient at higher risk for suicide.

Pointing out glaring contradictions of the patient's psyche can be particularly risky to the patient's well being.

Not genuinely caring about the patient's welfare, coupled with other factors, can serve to inch them toward the side of suicidal consideration.

If a therapist is consistently insensitive and or judgmental to a patient's regrets or losses, it can lead to hopeless despair.

CHAPTER 15

Further guidance for "clinical success" didn't appear on the flyer, but rather was addressed in case conference by Mischen:

"To put it succinctly," she said with a matter of fact tone, "as therapists, we should highlight the patient's mission to annihilate innocent beings, with the intent to stimulate and heighten the patient's moral conflict. Then, work to intensify feelings of shame in the Invader.

If that is not feasible due to their character structure, appeal to their grandiosity and narcissism. Identify their individual choice to stand alone outside of the dictated mission and end their life as they see fit. They would then be an admired being, respected for their greatness by choosing their own destiny. The finer details on manipulating these patients can be addressed in supervision, or at the next case conference. Please note that readings on 'gaslighting' can be invaluable."

CHAPTER 16

Some therapists had yet to face their moment. The following session was shared at case conference.

Dr. Duggin-

How are you?

Ali-

I'm sad Dr. Duggin

Dr. Duggin-

Sad?

Ali-

Yes, sad. It took months to open up. Now that I have, it makes me so sad.

Dr. Duggin-

How is it to admit your purpose here on Earth?

Ali-

I feel terrible about it. I couldn't be more ashamed. I said it before I'll say it again. I did not choose this. I was drafted for service and couldn't claim what you call, a conscientious objector. I could have lost my professional license or been jailed.

Dr. Duggin-

I understand Ali.

Ali-

I feel close to you, I wouldn't bring harm to you or anyone else. Even though both our species can be aggressive and murderous, humans can be so real, so loving. My home is not like that. I am deeply dispirited.

Dr. Duggin-

You feel defeated and ashamed.

Ali-

Yes, very strongly.

Dr. Duggin-

I get what you're saying and feel sympathetic. But I think you can understand that with such a malevolent plan, I have to protect myself, and my people from being tricked.

I feel you're genuine, but how can I really know? Look at how proficient your kind is with changing your bodies and learning our language and culture. How do I truly know that your appealing statements are not just a ruse to *rope a dope* me in.

Ali-

Yes, that's my point. Even though I am sincere, you could never know for sure. That just adds another layer to my isolation and my pain.

Silence.

Ali-

Now we both know what needs to be done. And please, don't feel guilty after I'm gone. I've been on this planet long enough to know how guilt can imprison people. This is not your doing. The leaders of my world put me in this situation by crafting such a hideous plan. It's clear to me now. I accept my destiny.

Dr. Duggin-

Have you chosen a method?

Ali-

Yes, one that is painless as well as foolproof. No half measures for me.

Dr. Duggin-

I see.

Ali-

I need to act directly. Contrary to your saying that suicide is a permanent solution to a temporary problem, this permanent solution will eliminate a permanent problem. I wouldn't be able to live with myself if I didn't do my part to stop the genocide. Unfortunately I can't live with myself either way, but I know this is right. I do hope that others of my ilk will follow in my footsteps.

Dr. Duggin-

I share your hope. I should also tell you that your selfless action will not go unnoticed.

Ali-

What do you mean?

Dr. Duggin-

It takes a lot of heart and courage to sacrifice your life for us here on Planet Earth. I tell you that to ease your mind some, but don't misunderstand the need for you to follow through.

Ali-

I understand, thank you.

Dr. Duggin-

Goodbye, Ali.

As the door closed, Dr. Mary Duggin momentarily welled up, truly feeling sorry for her. Seconds later, contrary feelings surfaced as she felt satisfied over her imminent "therapeutic success." A short time later, deeper feelings of angry resolve filled her as she thought of the Alien threat still posed to her family, her country and to the human race.

CHAPTER 17

Several days later, Mischen peeked her head into Ms. Wynne's office. "Good morning Lucy, do you have a moment?"

She quickly clicked off of Angry Birds. "Sure, Mischen."

"I have been remiss not speaking with you earlier," Mischen said as she sat comfortably in the patient's chair.

"You're talking about my getting upset at the case conference yes?"

"Yes." Mischen replied.

"It is me who should have spoken to you. I'm sorry. So much has been going on. I 'm upset because this whole Alien thing has hit me close to home."

"Oh? How so?" Mischen said, as her field of emotional receptivity instinctively widened.

Ms. Wynne paused before replying, "My daughter Juliet is dating an Alien."

"Gott in himmel! I am *so* sorry to hear of this," exclaimed Mischen.

Ms. Wynne shook her head in disbelief, "It's beyond imagination. Feeling it kills me."

"It must be so difficult," Mischen said sympathetically.

Silence.

"It is doubly hard 'cause I can't tell her. She can be stubborn and defiant and is more likely to marry him if I tell her he's an Alien," lamented Ms. Wynne.

"I imagine you're burning inside over this," said Mischen.

"I am," replied Ms. Wynne holding her head high to stave off tears. "I...I...can't talk more, I have 5 patients coming in and two are Aliens. I want to be emotionally prepared."

Mischen slowly pushed herself up to stand. "I understand. You know I'm available anytime."

"That's good, because I may in fact call upon you."

CHAPTER 18

Over the next 9 weeks staff at 'Caring Folks' experienced a multitude of feelings. Never before had clinicians faced such a scenario. But despite the shocking shift to their antithetical mission, they remained true to themselves, their profession and their leader Mischen.

First, protocol was established. Any suspicion of a patient being an Alien was accompanied by evidence and brought to a vote. Should there be a 12 for 12 vote of guilt, the grim and distressing duty of facilitating the Alien's demise would follow. Again and again, the staff's empathic attunement proved invaluable to their internal reorientation.

Although Mischen noted progress, she was quite aware the window of opportunity was closing. She knew it was highly unlikely all Aliens would be eliminated, because after all, they weren't all in treatment. Unless the Few were to make a powerful statement to the Alien's leader, the Invasion would be at high risk to expand across the globe.

Mischen often thought of her parents, as well as the millions of others who were subject to inconceivable torment. She recalled a fragment of a poem, "For every hair on your head, somebody endured one struggle, one pain, one death."

CHAPTER 19

The next morning was *not unusual*. Both woke up with the sun, had a cup of coffee and felt hungry for something more. Since this particular Sunday morning was so bright and inviting, they both went to town for breakfast. Although they had never met, their actions shadowed one another. Sitting at the counter of Monk's

Cafe, she ordered eggs, sunny side up. He ordered an omelette with everything. She left a generous tip, while he stiffed the kind waitress. After paying the cashier, they arrived at the exit simultaneously. He stepped forward first, without holding the door for her. As she stepped out, he was lighting a cigarette. Looking up, Mischen saw him begin to cross the busy intersection, apparently unaware of the truck barreling down upon him. She gasped and aggressively put her arm out, stopping him just in time.

"Oh, my God," she uttered, deeply shaken over the close call. He seemed unfazed.

"You almost got killed!" she exclaimed as their eyes met for the first time.

He responded, "Nothing to worry about, I'd have been fine."

"But the truck was inches away from you!" she implored.

He chuckled, "You all worry too much about that kind of thing." Then he smiled in a cocky way stating, "Such worries are for mortals!" He threw back his head and let go a loud, eerie laugh. Even as he was laughing he realized this was not good for the cause and quickly regained his reserve.

Mischen shuddered momentarily, then lowered her gaze and saw his flawed hand. "He's an Invader," she said to herself. Mischen had met Aliens many times before, but this chance meeting was in neutral territory, on the innocent corner of Pasture Lane and White Bird Road. The reality of the Invasion suddenly intensified. She quickly contained her feelings seizing an opportunity.

Konn Jimm was seeking opportunity as well, but for a different reason. He apologized to Mischen for scaring her and thanked her for being concerned.

"I know you just had breakfast, but let me make it up to you, can I buy you a cup of coffee? There's a place around the corner." Mischen accepted his offer.

For close to an hour they both conversed with entirely different agendas. Mischen figured out his motives early.

"I am new to this area and would love to have a young lady show me around town." Listening to his smooth talk, she could feel the otherness of his being. Her initial anxiety was replaced by disgust and hate. The longer they spoke, the more her suspicions grew.

She wondered, "Is this their leader? I feel he is, but have no proof." She recalled the leaders name from when she met B Arnold. Mischen mustered up the courage to ask, cautioning her self to not exhibit emotion. Plenty of professional practice assisted, as she received his response.

"Konn Jimm" he replied, as he thrust out his hand to shake hers. As she shook it, she looked deeply into his eyes, galvanizing her resolve. She coldly swore to herself, "I will eliminate you and your army of killers!"

CHAPTER 20

They agreed to meet the next day at the edge of town. Konn Jimm thought he was meeting Mischen's niece, but Mischen had other plans. As he stepped out of his car, three burly men duct taped his mouth, covered him in burlap, and bundled him into the basement of a nearby building.

Initially, Konn Jimm appeared to be shaken up. But Mischen did not succumb to feeling an iota of compassion for him. As his head covering was lifted he grimaced, shook his head, and made a cursory attempt to muscle the ropes that tied him to the chair.

Mischen quieted him. "You know there's no reason to be concerned about your welfare. We both know your existence cannot be compromised. If we take off the tape will you listen and not yell?" He shook his head affirmatively and took a deep breath as the tape was torn away.

"We understand that you have come here from a faraway world for the purpose of genocide. Are you going to deny that?"

"I plead the 5th" Konn Jimm said with a smirk on his face. Mischen felt like slapping him, but contained herself.

For the next 45 minutes, Mischen was part therapist, part mother, part interrogator and part soldier.

She focused on conveying to her captive a sense of desperation. She sought out feelings of shame by confronting the cold-blooded disconnect of invading anothers' world to commit mass murder. She made it clear that suicide was his only recourse. Nothing short of that would be accepted. Never before had Konn Jimm ever considered taking his life.

Mischen went to Caring Folks to give him time to accept his fate. Although she knew that his suicide would successfully decapitate the mission, he may not agree, so she knew to consider other strategies.

Two hours later she returned to Konn Jimm.

"What have you decided?" Mischen said coldly.

He replied, "I understand what we spoke about, I've seen the light, you are right. I'll write a note in my native language ordering my troops to leave at noon tomorrow.

But I ask that you spare my life. I have a family just as you do. This Invasion was not my idea. I was just following orders. I didn't volunteer. I was drafted for this mission. Let me go home with the others and I'll swear off any idea of hurting humans.

Besides, you'll need a voice in my homeland to reason for peaceful relations with other civilizations."

Mischen listened intently. She did sense sincerity, yet recalled with clarity the times she was fooled by a sociopath. Mischen fully understood the decision she faced. Should she trust him to abandon the war efforts and leave? Was it really necessary to insist upon his death? After all, he was offering his unconditional surrender as the leader of the incursion.

CHAPTER 21

Mischen drove outside the city to a grassy, tree lined meadow. She often visited the graves of her mother and father. The absence of their corporeal existence didn't lessen her connection with them.

They had their own painful journey, yet had found their way and lived honorable lives. Mischen was not without a deep understanding of their plight. For most of her life she reflected upon the movement that had been so evil.

The same unanswerable questions appeared again and again. "How could humans be so inhuman? Why did such horrible actions occur? How can losses so immense be mourned? What have we learned? How is mankind to move forward?"

Now *she* was facing questions that demanded answers for the sake of all mankind. Mischen wondered, "What would my parents think? What would they feel? What direction would they believe is right?"

Upon further reflection, Mischen's course of action became clean glass clear. She knew in her heart and mind what was right and proceeded ahead.

CHAPTER 22

The Aliens had a complex network of communication allowing for a number of contingencies.

The written directive of Konn Jimm was quickly circulated among the Aliens, proudly spearheaded by B Arnold. That next day at the designated time, Mischen and the Circle Few stood in their parking lot looking to the open sky, anxiously awaiting a sign of the Aliens' departure. Ten were there as Mr. Stryker was active for the cause elsewhere and Ms. Wynne was tending to a family matter.

At exactly 12 noon, a blinding flash of light blew through them like a powerful gust of wind, as a bright cloud of matter/energy whooshed from ground to **sky**. They looked at one another and erupted in joyous cries of jubilance. Ebullient hugging drew perplexed stares from passersby.

Mischen sighed deeply as she imagined the Invaders whizzing through space toward their home, leaving Earth and its people safe. She couldn't help but think of Konn Jimm returning to his own body form, embracing his family, yet having to admit defeat to his fellow beings. She wondered what that would be like for him…

CHAPTER 23

Before fully celebrating, Mischen had one more detail to attend to. She left her co-workers and drove the few miles to the building. She glanced up as she exited the car. Mr. Stryker informed her that no one had left or entered since yesterday.

Mischen had offered him assistance through a doctor known for this kind of thing. But as she opened the basement door it was quite apparent he had not asked for guidance, as his corpse was hanging directly in front of her. Silent and fixed, Konn Jimm's eyes looked directly into hers. Apparently he had thought out his last position, with the motivation to either shock Mischen or induce guilt. But she would have nothing to do with either.

She had accepted the reality months ago and had no conflict leading Konn Jimm to his demise. But Mischen had to admit it was odd to feel *satisfaction* over his death. Nonetheless, she was greatly relieved. Hours later she imagined that his physical position in death was his way of not dying alone.

A note was left accepting responsibility for taking his life and apologizing for any pain he brought to anyone. Nothing was said about the Invasion, as that was left in Mischen's hands.

CHAPTER 24

Unbeknownst to Mischen, the last Invader was racing to save a human, precariously hanging on the edge of a Californian land bridge.

Tony and Juliet were not unlike many young couples in love. Happiness, punctuated by intense conflicts, resulting in confusion, heartache and tears, was a pattern repeated as if following a predetermined behavioral script of DNA. The question, "Should we *stay* together?" certainly seemed normal enough, but it was the unspoken secret that deeply tore at them.

Juliet couldn't make sense of how Tony felt about her. At times, she could feel his love. At others, he'd repeat his mantra, "We're too different to make a life together." Tony just couldn't tell her the unfathomable truth: "I'm from outer space and we've come here to annihilate every living person!"

Juliet's mother prayed that her daughter would realize for herself. But Juliet's mind would not allow for the truth to be known. She was resolute and independent regarding matters of the heart, no doubt influenced by the early loss of her beloved father...

Being a single parent, Lucy Wynne has always been protective of her only child. Haunted by fears that her beloved Juliet would be a victim of the Invasion, she broke her oath to the Few. But as predicted, Juliet refused to accept the Alien idea, claiming her mother was just trying to "control her life."

CHAPTER 25

Their morning hike in the hills started with short, uphill steps, shared on a dusty trail. But following a particularly distressing trade of words, Juliet slipped from view as Tony was taking pictures of the valley.

He ran as soon as he noticed she was missing. There she was, fifty yards up the trail, holding desperately to the outside of a land bridge. Her hiking boots precipitously held to the edge of a lower rail, while her hands tightly clutched the metal beam above her head. Tony quickly reached her position on the bridge.

"Don't do this!" he cried.

"What *should* I do?" she replied.

"You have a life!"

"Without you, I have no life."

"That's not true. Grab my hand! You have me, we just can't stay together," Tony implored.

"Then life is not worth living," Juliet said sadly.

Suddenly, her foot slipped. Tony reached out and grabbed Juliet's hand just as her grip failed. He held tightly as he carefully stepped over the barrier between them, assuming the position on the bridge that she just held, while Juliet dangled over the abyss.

"Do not let go!" he barked.

Juliet was without words as she looked down at her near fate. He pulled her up and close. They kissed, joined as one.

Removed from their kiss, they gazed into one another's eyes. He said softly, "You must hear the truth, I'm not from here, I am..." Before he could say the word, Juliet said, "I know who you are, you don't have to say it."

At that instant, Tony's hiking boot slipped on the thin metal rail. Suddenly he began to plummet as she had moments before. Juliet deftly reached out and saved *him* from falling. He hung, suspended over the open space for what seemed to be an eternity. They were never closer. Both knew what was next.

"I will let go of your hand, but I will never let go of you," Tony said.

"You do love me," she said softly.

As their eyes were locked in love, she let him lessen his grip of her hand. Then, he intentionally let go and fell away, peacefully falling back into oblivion. He was gone. And so too was the last vestige of the greatest threat to mankind in recorded history.

CHAPTER 26

Back east, Mischen congratulated everyone for their wonderful work and then contacted the authorities. Various intelligence agencies interviewed the staff over several days. The debriefing was followed a week later with a private ceremony at the national park outside of town. Initially the pomp and pageantry of the occasion offered a last layer of profound relief to the most troubling time of their lives. However those feelings swiftly shifted when a long black limo quietly pulled up, and out stepped the President of the United States! The Few were bursting with pride when she bestowed to each of them the Presidential Medal Of Freedom. Nothing in their lives would ever rival that moment!

Near the end of the event, the Few were quite surprised to see Mr. Anthony Thacher, the kind man who just finished a 3-month state fiscal review of their clinic. But when the President introduced him as Mr. Thacher FBI agent, their jaws dropped in unison as their heads turned to Mischen. She, in turn, remained stoic, clapping her hands for the FBI and their support during the most challenging period of her life.

The official release of the thwarted attack was just days away. The President and her handlers were timing the news to maximize political benefit both nationally and globally.

When the news was released, the gravity of the accomplishment was not lost on anyone. For weeks, *billions and billions* of people were feverishly exhilarated beyond words. Media and the masses alike idolized the Circle Few. Everyone, everywhere, drowned them in adoration. Despite the immense response, the Few maintained their professionalism at all times. Mischen did her best to be empathic to the masses, feeding them every tidbit of truth they so hungrily desired.

Mischen had struck an agreement with the FBI, the major news carriers and interested groups at large, that she and the staff would be available for inquiries for 40 days. After which, "The Darling Dozen," would have privacy and their lives would go back to normalcy. Despite, or perhaps because of global adulation, their wish was granted.

The shared jubilation across country and continent ushered in a long epoch of civility unparalleled in human history. It particularly kindled a period of mutual respect between the media, those in notoriety and the masses.

CHAPTER 27

Slowly but steadily, Mischen began to withdraw as she reflected upon her life. She found herself spending more time with her grandchildren. At 5 years of age the twins adored their Grandma, so it made perfect sense to them that everyone else did too!

Mischen left instructions for the week after their Bar and Bat Mitzvah that her grandchildren would receive a first hand video accounting of the Invasion and the humanity that saved the world. And as the daughter of two survivors, Mischen shared their family's history of suffering and courage that emerged from the horror of the Holocaust. It was important to preserve for the future what had transpired in the past.

CHAPTER 28

As the 40-day boundary grew to a close, Mischen attended one last event in her honor. Despite her period of self-reflection, she was fully present at the dinner, accepting the enormous praise heaped upon her.

She left the event feeling *so right*. Driving along the dark country road she couldn't resist briefly turning off her car lights, just as her Dad did many years before.

As Mischen approached her home she turned inward. Stepping out of her car, she looked at the spacious starry night. She didn't even think of them.

The night was dark as the moon was turning elsewhere. Walking to her door, Mischen could hear the rustling winter leaves as a gentle breeze crossed in front of her.

Feeling her parents' presence, she slid her key into the lock. They entered, staying with her as the door snapped shut.

Mischen took great pleasure in negotiating the unlit rooms with astute exactness, as she quietly prepared for a long restful sleep. Slipping between the white sheets of her bed, Mischen was enclosed by the black of night. She shut her eyes and envisioned white cumulus clouds billowing in a blue summer sky. Laying her head back, she admired the lofty and royal clouds drifting serenely in her mind's sky. Their eloquence and grace blurred with Mischen as they silently moved forward, marking time so gently. Light and free, she drifted in their white, touching the face of divine existence.

Profoundly content and in perfect peace, Mischen held in her heart of hearts her Mom and Dad, and those who suffered so, eight decades past. There were no words as she folded her hands upon her chest, fully embracing the dark and the light within.

The End

A Time To Reflect

Walking from room to room isn't as straightforward as one would imagine. JJ and Jill shuffle sideways in their attic bedroom because the landlord has yet to build the promised dormer. Every painful conk on the head reminds them that they are not homeowners. That aside, the shape of their apartment isn't the only thing uneven and tilted, as Jill's father is an active alcoholic whose behavior is at best, unpredictable.

Jill and her family have suffered in various ways, in a multitude of situations. Her father's drinking and mother's enabling, contribute to Jill's commitment fears and unhealthy dependency. As for JJ, he's had *his* share of issues, having come into the world with only half the assets of other newborns.

Jill spent the afternoon on a recliner, watching television talk shows and worrying about her relationship with JJ. After several hours she began to doze off, only to be awakened by a cadence of steps. She looked up at the sound of jostling keys. As JJ stepped into the living room, Jill perked up, carefully crafting her tone to hide her mistrust.

"Oh, hi hon. Where were you?"

"I was with my Aunt Gladys," he said, walking directly to his laptop.

Jill narrowed her eyes, "You were just there last week, why are you seeing her so much?"

"I told you, she's helping me put together my past. She's got a great memory and knows neighbors from my childhood."

"Oh good." Jill said, calmer by his report.

Within a minute JJ was totally absorbed by a screen, leaving Jill insecure.

"Honey? What are you doing?...Hon?" "What?" he replied with a hint of annoyance.

"You're on the computer again? Not another night," she moaned, "it takes so much time from us."

"I am trying to find a psychotherapist. It's not easy finding the right one."

She leaned, peering over his shoulder. "You're looking for a therapist in California?"

"Yes, I want to find the right one. You don't just go to *any* therapist you know," he said with a sense of pride. "I can understand, but 3000 miles away?" "Huh?" muttered JJ.

"I said. You're looking for a therapist 3000 miles away." "Yes, I am."

"I can't believe this! You're going all the way to California just to be in therapy? That's ridiculous! I don't get it! It makes no sense."

JJ said nothing.

"What will that mean for us? Am I going too, or is it over? Why do you always do this to me?"

JJ turned and looked directly into her eyes, "I can't answer a bunch of questions now. However, I *can* say I love you. I want our relationship. But yes, I am seeking a therapist in California," he emphasized. "That's enough about that, c'mere and give me a kiss."

"No. I don't kiss people who leave me hanging after 3 years."

JJ grunted, leaving the next several days distant between them. Their orbits continued to cross without concert until love and a beautiful day brought them together.

Sitting on a park bench they leaned into the other's center and held hands. Soaking in the sun's warmth, they admired the work of the wind. Green leaves shook and swayed as the breeze yielded an occasional gust. During a particularly intense rush of wind, JJ blurted, "I found him."

"Found who?"

"I found my future psychotherapist." "Really? Where is he?" Jill asked with curiosity. "Huntington Beach, California."

Jill began to cry. "Are you serious? You're actually gonna leave me?"

"I have to go. I have no choice. And it makes no sense for you to come. I just need to deal with my father leaving me. You know that's an issue for me."

Gathering herself she responded, "Hon, I understand you have to confront that demon, but California?"

"That's exactly where I need to go."

"How long will you be there? Will we keep our place? Will you come back? Please come back." She pressed close to him as he absently patted her hand.

"I'm not going for years, just long enough to work it out. It's more important than you realize. Some day you'll understand."

"Do you promise?"

"Yes, I promise."

The rest of the day was quiet, as each was busy 'California Dreamin,' JJ with his wishes, Jill with her fears. That night, they arrived home at the same time. Getting out of their cars JJ smiled, which Jill mocked in return. Immediately feeling guilty, Jill smiled at JJ, which he then ignored.

Breaking the tension between them occurred naturally when the hall credenza received their keys with a mutual clink of joined.

A few minutes passed. "Jill?"

"Yes, JJ."

"I made the phone call today." "What phone call?"

"I spoke to his secretary, he's got a free hour. I'm set for 2 weeks from Thursday."

Jill burst into tears. This time JJ went to her side, genuinely consoling her.

"I promise you, I'll be back. You'll understand when I return. Then we'll move forward. But right now you have to accept that I need to do this."

Fighting back tears she replied, "I understand."

He held her until she let go of him, then said, "Can you help me pack?"

"Sure. Did you tell work yet?"

"Yes, I quit. I told them I wouldn't be back." "Why? Why would you close that off?"

"I'm starting a new direction when I get back." "What direction?"

"I don't know, I'll know when I get back." "Oh, just like that!"

"Yup."

For the next 3 days JJ prepared for his trip. Driving cross-country to march through his issues raised JJ's anxiety. Nevertheless, he was soothed with the knowledge that his constant companion would always be with him. Music. Wonderful, wonderful, music. Music would never fail him.

His van had a cooler in the front and a mattress in the back. In between, were the songs he loved, songs that had carried him through the days and nights of his fatherless life.

After goodbyes to Jill and his Mom, he took seminal steps forward. At the turn of his car key, *The Seventh Sojourn*, by The Moody Blues, escorted him on his way.

JJ chose to shadow Route 80 and capitalize on recent technology. He had purchased the compatible hardware and became among the first to experience, *Signs, Signs, Everywhere A Sign*, (SSES) project. Highways adjacent to Route 80 were recently cleared of all lights, signs and advertisements. No longer would they clutter the beautiful coast-to-coast scenery.

Instead, all signs were projected digitally, by way of wi-fi, from the dashboard, to the inside of the custom treated windshield. As vehicles drove forward, images appeared and disappeared, ruled by GPS and the specific locale. Drivers chose different levels of sign-free views. Since he had no immediate purchasing needs, JJ chose the "scenic view," blocking all advertisements and all unnecessary signs. Of course, any vital notices appeared when indicated. JJ drove on, surrounded by green, as he viewed a pristine America unfettered by the ruinous view of money seeking money.

Miles ahead, became miles behind, as the numbers added up and the music played on. With every change of CD, he thought of his Mom, a master of weaving music and moments. All his life she healed his heart with song, filling the painful cavity left by his father's absence. Recollections of warmth led to, *Sea Of Joy*, by Blind Faith.

As JJ sped on, the day's light was squeezed from the sky, as the black night took hold. JJ knowingly smiled, secure with his hopes as he drove alone on *Highway 61*.

Several days later JJ arrived in southern California, at the modest, yet attractive, village where his psychotherapist had his office. He drove a few minutes before reaching the home that housed the room he rented online. His landlord was sitting on her porch, as if she had been waiting for days.

They met on the cracked sidewalk near the driveway. Ten seconds of tightness twisted, till Ben Franklin's face appeared in numbers. Emotional knots unraveled with an ease of yes, as her wariness slid to a smile. JJ mused to himself, "She must be a patriot!"

That next day he arrived at his first psychotherapy appointment. He nervously took a seat in the waiting room. There, directly in front of him hung Wassily Kandinsky's Yellow Red Blue painting, one of JJ's all time favorites. Initially, he felt a feeling of being with a familiar friend, but that quickly shifted to a queasy discomfort.

JJ was startled when the door suddenly opened and a middle-aged woman came out weeping. Moments later, out stepped Dr. Jonathon Jack. He greeted JJ in a cordial manner. They sat facing each other with a gulf between them greater than mere measure.

"So JJ, although we spoke briefly on the phone, tell me more fully what brings you here?"

JJ said nothing as his eyes darted from side to side. He then said flatly, "I'm here because I didn't have an easy childhood. It affects me now in my adult life."

"Oh? In what way?"

"I feel distant to what goes on around me. Yet, when I am involved, I get frustrated and need to distance myself."

"I see, tell me more."

"I grew up with only one parent." "Oh?"

"I have my Mom, but my father was never in the picture. He's dead."

"I'm sorry to hear that. Did you know him at all?" "No."

Dr. Jack soon sensed JJ was reluctant to share about the father, so he redirected the focus. Otherwise the session seemed to go well, as JJ agreed to meet again on Monday.

The 4 days of waiting for JJ were marked with a fisherman's patience. *Willie and Leon* soothed his heart while he wandered the village in a dreamy state of nothing and nowhere.

Monday arrived without the anxious feelings of last week. Determined, he brought himself to the direction sought.

As he approached Dr. Jack's office, his eyes were drawn to surrounding greenery, posting hello from the rich brown earth. Climbing the unyielding red brick steps, he curved his hand around the upward slope of the wrought iron rail. Noticing the door seemed smaller than it did on Thursday, JJ randomly wondered if Dr. Jack owned the building.

Just then, a woman left the office. She was not crying. As JJ entered and sat down, he quickly said to Dr. Jack, "I have to clarify something."

Dr. Jack leaned forward with genuine interest.

"I know I told you my father's dead, but that's not true. He's alive, but is dead to me. He left my Mom and me and made no effort to contact us. He's dead to me 'cause he never made an effort to be a father."

"I see," Dr. Jack replied. "How has that been for you?"

"Not good. But I'm not ready to talk about it. I just wanted you to hear the truth."

"Ok," Dr. Jack replied.

It was in this session that JJ and Dr. Jack agreed to accelerate the therapy by meeting twice a week. Over the next few weeks JJ spoke broadly about his life. Topics ranged from his lack of career direction, to his relationship with Jill and to his periodic impulsivity.

JJ was quite aware he was relating to Dr. Jack facts, but not feelings. He also noted that Dr. Jack was making an attempt to emotionally connect with him. This pleased JJ, but perhaps not for the usual reasons one would imagine.

Then, when the timing felt just right, JJ decided to address the absence of his father. Up to that point, Dr. Jack hadn't said much about JJ's loss. JJ decided to open up the topic by confronting Dr. Jack. "You haven't said anything about my deadbeat father. There's a part of me that thinks you're trying to ignore my abandonment."

"I'm sorry you feel that way JJ. I was respecting your wish. I was waiting for you to be ready..."

"Well, I'm ready now," JJ said firmly. "I told you that my father abandoned us. He was never there for my Mother and never there for me. No call, no card, no money, no contact, no connection whatsoever. What kind of man would do that to his own flesh and blood?"

"How did that make you feel?" asked Dr. Jack.

"Can't you use your imagination? How do *you* think a little boy would feel?"

"There's a range of feelings that someone may feel, I'm trying to understand yours."

Silence.

"Maybe there's some reason why he did..." stumbled Dr. Jack.

JJ glared at him, "Are you defending him? Are you suggesting it was my fault for being born?"

"No, I am just saying, for instance, maybe he lost contact or God forbid, perhaps he died..."

JJ did not let him finish, "In this day and age of the internet, people can find whoever they're looking for. I know for a fact he is alive and yet shows no effort to understand!"

"How do you know he's alive?" Dr. Jack asked, attempting to hide his anxiety and surprise over JJ's intensity.

"Listen to me! That's irrelevant! I am serious. I have driven 3000 miles and I want an answer! How can a father abandon his own son?"

"I can't say JJ."

"Would you agree that he is selfish and heartless?"

"I am sure it is very painful as you have mentioned..."

"Why do you go back to me, I'm asking you about my father!"

"I'm not going to defend him and I can understand your deep feelings of abandonment. Yet you never can know what may have been going on for him."

"*For him!* How would his needs as an adult be more important than a helpless vulnerable child? *For him!* Can you imagine what it felt like to be relentlessly teased for not having a father? Every year I hoped beyond all hope that my Dad would show up for Christmas. That's all I ever wanted! Yet every year I was heartbroken, again and again. Wouldn't that be more important than anything my so-called father might be going through?"

"Yes, JJ it would be. You're right. I feel your pain. I am very sorry. I truly am."

Time had run out. As JJ stood, Dr. Jack went to open the door as was customary with the office setup. But JJ would not allow it.

Decisively he acted, leaving the door wide open like the gaping hole of a wound.

Dr. Jack was stunned. He sat on the couch as silence consumed the room. A silence that felt uniquely strange. Feelings he had never felt before.

Thoroughly trained, with decades of experience as a therapist, Dr. Jack knew not to let his personal feelings confound the process of psychotherapy. But at that moment Dr. Jack's personal and professional life felt blurred, leaving him confused and anxious.

Dr. Jack had to admit that as a young man in his early teens, his girlfriend had become pregnant. More than that he did not know. Also unknown, was if his father's sudden pastoral assignment was truly the reason his family hurriedly left for California. Surely, shame insured that as a young teen it was never spoken of again.

Sitting in the stillness, he stared out at the empty grey sky. No one could hear his thoughts. "Is this just a reminder for me, borne out of associative guilt? Or is it possible that this is my son? What would be the chances of that? If he is my son, does he know it? Has he perhaps known that I am his Father and orchestrated all of this?"

Dr. Jack needed to clarify the truth. "If JJ isn't my son the therapy needs to get back on track, but if we are *father and son* we need to know it! I must talk to him. This must be resolved. We cannot proceed until I speak with him."

Waiting 3 days for their next session was painfully difficult for Dr. Jack. After all, if JJ was his son he would be Dr. Jack's only child, satisfying deep wishes quietly existing for many years.

Hope took hold as time grew close. Dr. Jack felt an excitement he had never felt as an adult. He looked forward to the next appointment like a child who just can't wait for a holiday to arrive. Dr. Jack bathed in the feelings of his thoughts, "If he is my son there'll be so much to talk about, so much to share and so much to mend."

When Thursday finally arrived Dr. Jack woke up feeling enthused that this young man might be his son! Feeling eager to see him, Dr. Jack excitedly arrived early to his office. JJ was his first appointment of the day.

As Dr. Jack waited, his eyes became fixated on the clock. After just a few minutes a multitude of feelings mounted. At 15 minutes of no arrival, he began to imagine a list of reasons for JJ's lateness. They all rested upon the idea JJ would be arriving momentarily. After 25 minutes he thought to himself that something might have happened to JJ.

"You never know," said Dr. Jack reassuring himself, "maybe he mixed up the day or ran out of gas. I'll call if I don't hear from him in an hour or two." 15 minutes hadn't passed before Dr. Jack made the call. To his further bewilderment, JJ's phone was no longer in service. Naturally, as a therapist, Dr. Jack wondered, "Was it something that I said?"

Emptiness filled his weekend, as Dr. Jack felt disconnected and alone. He yearned to see JJ's face again. A slight tick upward of hope rose on Monday, as Dr. Jack prayed JJ would attend.

But he did not.

Despite 20 years of maintaining strict therapeutic boundaries, Dr. Jack found himself driving to the address JJ had left for an emergency contact. Finding the house easily he approached an older woman watering the yard.

"Hello!" Dr. Jack boomed across the spotty, sand marked lawn. She quickly secured a pint in her pocket and lifted her head. But before she could respond, Dr. Jack said, "I'm looking for a young man who lives here."

"No young man here. There *was* a young man, but he left over a week ago." She added, "Nice young man, from back east. JJ was his name."

"Yeah, that's him," Dr. Jack said with a hint of hope in his voice. "Yeah, Jackson was his name, Jackson John. Who are you? Are you his father? You sort of look alike, well, maybe not. JJ was a nice young man. What do *you* want?"

"I am his...well I should say, we worked together. Did he leave a phone number or forwarding address?"

"No."

That single syllable was a body blow Dr. Jack will never forget. He retreated quickly to his car. Tears arrived before he could open the door. His mind throbbed like a bleeding wound, as his thoughts pounded within.

"Why would he just disappear? Didn't he want to share being father and son? He was just here and now he's gone. We could have connected, could have had a relationship. I never got to say anything to my son as a father. This is so devastating! Why would he do this?"

Suddenly, years of denial fell away. His heart ached as it came to him. "Oh, God, oh no, of course." Painfully he cried out, dissolving into tears. "I am so sorry. Forgive me! Forgive me!"

But Jackson was not there to hear him. He was driving leisurely through the upper Midwest while listening to *Abbey Road*. Rock formations attracted him as he drove past a dirt road. The cut off was tight, but he turned in time as a body of blue came to view. Jackson had discovered a box canyon lake formed by an ancient glacier. Jagged rock walls, perfectly reflected in the pristine waters, circularly bordered the open sky. Jackson was deeply moved by the reflection, as the two images were nearly indistinguishable.

Shedding his clothes, he immersed himself in the cool and purifying water. Jackson serenely swam the backstroke, peering into the clear blue sky of deep, dreaming of the future.

Moved by the earth and sky, he had absently left his car door open with speakers sailing their song to the open air.

From a distance he could hear,

"And, in the end, the love you..."

The End

Noble Shepherd, A Common Man

I was born of common folk. For generations we have lived a good clean life. I married young, found a solid position at Woolworth's and worked hard for 35 years to provide for my loved ones. My wife and I have been dedicated to our family and have always thanked God through prayer for the simple pleasures of life: family, health, and our fortunate bounty.

Although I would have liked to leave "footprints" here on earth, I've never really stood out, nor did any key opportunity come my way. I can't deny that like many people, I have had dreams, but at 64 years of age, I accept things as they are. I am who I am. I've always believed my legacy would be devotion to family, community and Church.

My family never took anything for granted. We've always appreciated the natural beauty surrounding us. As each day slips away, we watch the sun ebb out of the sky by the turn of the Earth. We cherish the colors and patterns of the heavens, sketched upon our hearts by God Himself.

My Grandma used to say that God creates pleasing sunsets to comfort folks as they face the dark and unknown night.

Me, I've always had two fears. One is not living a worthy life. The other, since we live in Nebraska, is the threat of tornadoes. Although I have seen my fair share of them, God has always spared us the pain and suffering of sharing the same space with one.

In our later years, my dear wife and I took a trip we had dreamt about for a lifetime. We timed it to commemorate the 300th anniversary of my ancestors arriving from England. We so enjoyed touring the port they left from centuries before.

At the tail end of our vacation I chose to be a bit daring. Many years ago my uncle gave me a ride on his motorcycle. I recall how frightened I was. Yet, I always wanted to ride again. So on our last day—despite my bride's wishes to the contrary—I rented a motorcycle for 2 hours of wind in my face pleasure.

It was May 13th 1935 and I was riding on a narrow tree-lined trail in Dorset, when suddenly I saw a serviceman on a motorcycle speeding across my forward direction. Despite my best efforts, I collided with the chap.

Although the impact was powerful, I remember the moment that rendered me unconscious. After a time, I regained my awareness and mounted my bike. There was no sign of the man I struck.

As I rode on, I was bewildered that the roads had no traffic and no one was anywhere. Down the road some I noticed a sign for a rest stop, so I followed the arrow to the turnoff, and parked my bike. I was surprised to see the building was closed and that it looked shadowy and odd. Behind the rest stop were several drab, Army barracks-like buildings, surrounded by a tall grove of trees.

Suddenly, I heard a commotion. Looking to my right, I was dumb struck frozen! There was my Mother and Grandmother, coming to greet me! The fact they had died some years before didn't hinder their enthusiasm. Moment's later, other friends and family from my past trickled out to see me. Each had died some time ago, yet now stood in front of me seemingly alive and well and in the flesh! I blurted out, "What the...? Am I in Heaven? Am I dreaming? How is this possible?"

They did not respond as the warm reunion drowned out my questions. I yielded to their feelings and shared the joy. In a matter of minutes though, they looked tired and became quiet. My mother put her hand in mine and led me to her dwelling, as the others filtered away.

As we entered, I went to sit down but my Mom kept hugging me. I pried myself from her grip. I just had to know!

"Mom, is this Heaven? Have I died?"

"Yes, it seems so."

"Oh my God!" Noble said with wide eyes and a hard swallow. He added, "Not that it isn't great to see you, Grandma and everyone else, but I'm not happy my time on earth is over."

"I understand...we all dream of being home. But in our heart of hearts we yield to the will of God."

Noble and his Mom looked away feeling comforted, but sad.

"But Mom, if this is Heaven, why is everything so drab and run down? This doesn't look like Heaven."

Noble's Mom touched his arm reassuringly, "I'm sorry to have to tell you, but...Heaven sucks honey."

"Mother! You've never used that word!" "Everyone says it...it's true, Heaven sucks."

"How? Why? Where's God and why is it like this?"

"I'll say more later. I need to sleep."

"Yeah, and what's that about, everyone looking so tired? Isn't it still daytime?" Noble said peering out the window for the Sun. "Hey, where's the Sun? I don't see it. The lighting is weird."

"No more now honey," his Mom said wearily. Noble smiled, reflecting on the past. "Yeah, just like you used to say when I was little, *tomorrow is another day.*" They walked away feeling warmly connected.

Noble wandered about till gravitating to the base of a large fig tree. He collapsed into its support, as he longed for loved ones at home.

Noble wept.

When Noble's Mom woke up, they shared a meager meal culled from a modest garden. Then they went outside and sat on a bench. Mary wore the expression of a concerned parent protecting her child from a disturbing reality. Yet arguably the time had come to let go, as Noble *was* in the seventh decade of his life.

Noble's Mom shared, "I'm sorry. My mind isn't together. I get so tired. This will help..."

Mary carefully took pages from an odd sleeve of parchment. Resting them on her lap, she took a deep breath and read them slowly, but clearly.

"In the beginning God created Heaven and Earth. Initially the human population was few in number. But as more people were born and died, God tried to create a Heavenly Home for each deceased. Having room to house everyone became a problem. Equally important was living near loved ones, so God arranged for parents and grandparents to live directly behind the deceased branching back vertically, while friends were located next door extending horizontally.

But it became confusing. As more and more family and friends were housed, generations widened, messing up God's design. Like multiple chess games on the same board, the placement of people became a problem. God didn't know what to do. He wanted to provide a Heavenly experience without relying on mass transit for people to see loved ones"

"This is so strange," Noble said shaking his head in disbelief. "What else do you know?"

"There is much Noble," she said, "Can you read? I'm weary." "Sure, Mom," Noble said as he relieved the papers from her hands and read on.

"As you can imagine, God being God, He's had some serious expectations laid upon Him. But despite the fact He *is* God, some think He has difficulties making decisions. Yes, the Almighty is capable of whipping up worlds at the drop of a crown, but it's not just about power and miracles, it's also about judgment."

Noble paused as his jaw dropped, as this was so *beyond*.

He continued, "Some time ago God arrived at a solution for His placement of people problem. Little did He know, it would be the last important decision He'd make for many clouds to come."

Noble stopped and asked "What kind of solution?" His mother did not respond.

Noble held the next page gently between his fingers, with a who-knows-what I'm going to read next look on his face.

Fueled by her loving instincts, Mary Shepherd mustered up the energy and asked to read more. Noble yielded.

"So to fix the problem of loved ones in Heaven and their location to each other, God made divisibility."

Noble looked up and exclaimed, "What in Lord's name is divisibility?"

Mary read on, "Divisibility is God's plan. As each new arrival settles in to Heaven, God creates multiple copies of them. Each copy of a person *is* the exact person. The resulting 'person version' is known as a 'divisible.' The purpose is for each person and their copies to be with a family member in one location in Heaven and with different friends or family at another."

"This is *beyond imagination!*" Noble said as he repeatedly shook his head.

She continued to read, "God spreads divisibles across Heaven in specific strategic locales. A diverse distribution of dopplegangers designed to deliver endearment."

"*Holy Moses* who wrote that!"

"There's more," said Noble's mother.

"The bad part is that God didn't expect that each divided person would be weaker, a shallow copy of themself. For instance, if a person has 10 loved ones, he is divided by divisibility into 10 copies of himself. But divisibles lack the intensity of their original self. They get tired easily, feel lifeless and their minds lack the depth they once had."

"Is that why you and the others seem, no offense to you Mom, fatigued and flat?"

"Yes."

"Well then how are you relating all this to me in a knowing manner?"

"I read the words, but lose the point. It fades fast."

"Is that going to happen to me, will I be divisibilized?"

"I think so."

"Mom, what are those papers you're reading from?"

"I can't talk more. I'm dead tired..."

While his mother slept, Noble walked freely about. He was struck by the endless rows of dull and drab dwellings, each housing bunk beds with tattered blankets and undecorated walls. No photos were evident and there was no sign of electricity anywhere. Clothes lacked imagination and were bereft of artistic line or design.

From the soft cloud-like support under his feet, to the pale sky above, a colorless world framed the flat, expressionless faces that walked emptily from one place to another. There appeared to be no meaning or direction to their movement. Noble found Heaven depressing and disturbing.

Earlier gave way to later, as Noble struggled to take in the reality around him. He soon found himself again looking into the worn face of his mother. She pressed on, as she strained to look into his eyes.

"You asked about these...these words," she said wearily shaking the papers. "Hold on, where was I? Ahh, here..."

'These words tell us what is true. They are sacred. Many have contributed to their truth. Because divisibility has left us a bit feeble minded, we must write our beliefs down, so we don't forget them."

"But if everyone is so challenged where do these ideas come from?"

"One second, I have the verses for 'Newcomers.' Ah, here they are. 'When a newcomer arrives in the hereafter, there's a brief period to profit from their intact minds. The window is small, but the reward is large. Newcomers swiftly read previous writings and in some rare situations, they've met with God. Because we all are partitioned as per God's decree of divisibility, any knowledge is saved to these scrolls. These texts have become our gospel. They are a testament to our devotion to know."

"Wow."

Mary Shepherd read on, "But divisibility has been a failure. The mood in Heaven is dispirited and lifeless. Feeble or not, we all kno..."

Mary rested her mind for a short brief on the white cloud fluff drifting past her head. Noble patiently absorbed her peacefulness, noting the importance for sleep in the afterlife.

When she awoke, Noble helped her find her place and she read on. "When God realized His divisibility blunder, He was deeply ashamed causing an enormous blow to His self-esteem."

"In addition...where are they...oh...oh here they are, God was also greatly disappointed after giving mankind free will on earth. The wars, the pollution, the killing off of life forms, the general insensitivity, along with a crummy Heaven, all led to His inability to act."

"What do you mean?" asked Noble.

"Well...other papers speak of God being what's it called clinically oppressed."

"Clinically oppressed?"

"Sorry, that's not it, it's 'clinically depressed,' His mood is double bottom low. He can't motivate Himself to do anything. He is listless and emotionally paralyzed."

"I feel sorry for Him," Noble inserted. "Oddly, it reminds me of our good Pastor Bob Burgess. He preached to us that Man was created in God's image. We've all heard of God being an Angry God, a Loving God, a Forgiving God, and a Merciful God. Well apparently God has other attributes and dispositions previously believed to be limited to mankind."

Noble sighed as he scanned his surroundings. "So this is why Heaven is so run down and dismal."

"Yes."

"So where does this leave us?" Noble asked, wishing his Mom could offer hope.

"In limbo," she replied, as she turned and walked away. Noble followed his Mother to the bunks where he laid down for the first time since standing up post accident.

After a long sleep, Noble woke up feeling washed out, as if he was getting the flu. He dragged himself about, lacking his usual verve. Suddenly, with a visceral thud, he realized he was a victim of divisibility. Anger was recognized, however muted and unmoving. Without making a conscious decision he yielded to walking aimlessly, without reason or care.

It's unknown in earth time how long he languished as a *nowhere man,* in a nowhere land. One moment flowed to the next, with no measurement. Clock and calendar were absent, leaving no days or time to register.

Timelessness was not unknown in Noble's time on Earth. On occasion, he fell under its spell, by a sky of stars. Another time it was ushered in by the Sun reflecting off poplar leaves in the dead-still summer afternoon.

But this was different. The Heaven he now knew was empty and hollow. Even seeing lost loved ones was sadly marred by their lackluster existence. Folks, who had been filled with vitality and zest, were now diluted, mere watered down versions of their previous selves. A purposeless direction tore at Noble's heart as a Man. Eventually, other feelings began to take shape.

Although Noble had always followed society's laws and customs, something deep inside refused to spend eternity in a meaningless gray chamber of gloom.

Despite being weakened, or perhaps because of it, Noble was curious about his own divisibles. Then one day, he randomly ran across one of him. He had to admit it was quite unnerving to see himself! Noble spontaneously avoided him, feeling embarrassed and ashamed for unknown reasons.

Noble didn't understand why he and his double seemed so uncomfortable. Over time, he had other self-sightings with the same feelings. Then Noble reached out to other people about their indivisibles and they reported feeling similarly.

Noble observed that divisibles had become shameful isolators to their own selves. But despite feeling that way he was magnetically drawn to his copies. After several attempts, Noble was able to encourage one of him to engage in conversation.

At their first meeting the two of him simply shared where they resided and whom they knew nearby. During the second and third meetings, they spoke about avoidance and shame between alike divisibles.

Their talking sessions became more frequent, as Noble and Noble were determined to seek and keep knowledge of self and other. Thought and talk were put to paper swiftly, as frequent naps helped the brain regain.

He and him concluded that shame in seeing a self-copy is in part due to weakness from divisibility. Feeling weak was powerful enough, but seeing it in another self intensified inadequacies.

Soon, they brought another Noble into the fold. Working together helped combat the dumbing effects of divisibility. After a span, other insightful aspects were teased out.

No longer crippled by shame, the Nobles were liberated from self-estrangement. A resulting freer imagination added to understanding their own kind. At one quiet moment, the three of them suddenly laughed in unison, as they simultaneously thought, "If you could see yourself right now!" Each distinctly remembered when and with whom those words were said. No one needed to say it. That one common association strengthened their cause.

The Nobles' immense efforts deepened their understanding of divisibility driven behavior. It was noted that people protect their own mental cohesion by hiding facets of their identity from self-awareness. Seeing an exact copy of one's self, directly challenges human vulnerabilities.

It took courage, determination and a lot of naps to arrive at these conclusions and when they did, Noble, Noble and Noble embraced himself tightly, having arisen from the suffering of fragmentation.

Feeling like identical triplets, the Nobles sought out their "brothers" one by one. Avoidance by their divisibles was overcome by sheer perseverance.

Housing was arranged so every Noble Shepherd could stay together, as they routinely shared about Heaven, God and Earth. Then one particular night when Noble numbers peaked at 12, Noble's Mother Mary and family stayed at other barracks to encourage discussions. Through unquestionable common interests, the Nobles shared ideas and insights, while spreading the word as they knew it. In the end, the exhausting exchange was followed by a long rejuvenating sleep.

Upon awakening, they seemed *more like themselves* than they had in some time. It was then discovered, that one of them, Noble, had disappeared during the night.

They were initially concerned until a Noble conjectured that perhaps there was a connection between his disappearance and them feeling better. Had one Noble rejoined the remaining 11 that night? Had each become stronger because they were divided by one less?

This empowered the Nobles to seek any remaining selves. All the while, continued talks drew attention from neighbors who weren't Noble Shepherd. Although there had never been so many of the same divisible together in one place, no on-lookers ventured an ask.

Then, after many white clouds had drifted across the pale dome sky it was realized. The Nobles reversed divisibility! Predictable as an atomic clock, the prolonged proximity of head and heart led to the loss of a sleeping Shepherd.

Although initially sad, the Shepherds knew that every loss was really a gain. With each Noble gone, the remaining felt more restored and revitalized. Sadness brought strength. Infused with life, each Noble Shepherd felt increasingly free to make choices and seek meaning. A veritable resurrection from the dead!

'Twas a Noble cause, that non-Nobles were sought to seek themselves out. But because divisibility had weakened and shamed people so, many had fears and resisted risking their wellbeing.

All the same, Noble was empathetically patient with their anxieties. Listening in a crowd felt safer for many, so Noble took to the rooftops to preach the gospel of the undivided and regained self. The duplicates simply needed to have faith and believe! If they faced themselves with courage and trust, their everlasting life in Heaven could be Heavenly!

God being God, He was entirely aware of Noble and his words of wonder. He watched from a distance, as His depression wouldn't let Him off the proverbial couch of His Throne.

Then, suddenly, while reflecting upon Noble Shepherd, God felt a spark of life! He lifted His head and shook it briefly, shaking off His depressed stupor. It was as if God was waking from a long slumbering sleep.

The more He listened to the words of Noble, the more hopeful He became. Faith was rekindled, as God *believed* Noble could ease Heavenly suffering and provide purpose to the immortals.

Through Noble effort, Heaven's divided and lost souls were reunited with themselves. Selves became self, as the crippling effects of divisibility were disabled. Heaven's meaningless existence morphed to joyful connectedness, as the plague of divisibility was over.

Soon after, God called upon Noble Shepherd. He sought him not by words, but by will. Noble followed His calling and soon was in Gods'presence. Humbled and meek, Noble was filled with the awe of God and the bright light emanating from His being. Curiously, he thought God looked a little like Jimmy Stewart, but didn't say anything.

Noble Shepherd was known on Earth to be a good listener. People naturally felt understood as their world fit comfortably inside his. When God shared with Noble His experience of the last epoch, *He felt* understood. It was during a deep share that God realized the level of His loneliness.

An endearing acceptance by Noble, soothed Gods' anguished heart. The power of being heard by this brave and caring man helped lift *His* suffering. As His lost feelings of goodness and warmth found their way home, the Almighty imagined Heaven to be a happy place again.

Reflecting upon His recent depression, God became aware that Man did not fail His edict of free will. God had not been forsaken. But rather, *He* had lost faith in Man, as His expectations were just *too high.*

"After all," He thought to Himself, "men and women are just mortal beings seeking their way through a wilderness."

It became clear to Him, that Noble Shepherd *is* a successful example of free will! Upon that thought, God deeply exhaled. Like the sins of a novitiate at confession, the clouds obscuring the Sun lifted. He took a slow breath, filling His heart with hope and promise. God felt renewed and born again!

God recognized that along with Himself, Heaven and Earth had been brought back from the brink. They had been tightly entangled in the inactive bondage of guilt, shame and doubt.

Liberated from emotional paralysis, God was free to act on Earth. Accordingly, Earthlings believed (again) that God would answer their prayers. Souls in Heaven who were stalled in a purgatorial vehicle of meaninglessness, were re-routed to the road of happiness. God, Heaven and Earth were steered away from their sorrow and the pain of disconnection. All this accomplished, because a common man was willing to *face* himself.

The few who knew, regarded Noble Shepherd as a hero. Others felt he was a Man among Men. God recognized Noble Shepherd as a Savior!

With full respect, God smiled at the unity that came to mind:

Trinity.

God was so appreciative He decided to be generous to the Shepherds. God was shining bright with gratitude and enthusiasm, as He shared His divine decree that Noble, his wife, and their parents, along with the Shepherd children would all be together on Earth again. They would maintain what they know now and have the promise of a long life. To help insure that vow, God made each of them, 21 years of age.

When reunited, they were quite ecstatic and forever grateful, but Noble's wife had to ask, "Does God know what complications could arise from each member of a three generational family being 21 years old?"

Noble looked away saying, "No I don't think He does. Remember, He has no Grandmother, Grandfather, Aunt, Uncle, Cousin, Sister, Daughter or Brother. He's on the light side in the interpersonal realm. When it came to making us all 21, something went awry, God or no God."

Mrs. Shepherd nodded her head, "Yeah, I see what you mean. Even Earth's brightest exercise poor judgment, and we're made in God's image. Not unlike us, His judgment may not always be the best. Should I say something to Him?"

"No," said Noble, "It may hurt His feelings."

Meanwhile, the souls in Heaven were exercising *their* free will, quite freely. The immortals were excitedly alive with stunning vitality. A surging gush of creativity filled the air, as a *renaissance* burst forth. Arts emerged and buildings were built, as smiles and laughter punctuated a code of practicality. A warm glow of wholeness spread from within, as their proverb rang true:

"We're building an Earth, here in Heaven!"

The End

Blood Lines

Dr. Hue sits in his steel city office leafing through a book of Chinese Art. He lingers upon Zhao Mengfu, 1254-1322 and his painting, "A Man and His Horse In The Wind." Dr. Hue marvels at the divine moment of ordinary, captured 700 years ago and now on view for all, forever in time.

Dr. Hue is a highly respected psychotherapist who brings a broad perspective to the field. Decades of education, training and experience have woven a colorful fabric of care, changing a host of lives for the better.

However, nearly 2 years ago his work began to suffer. Dysfunction convened against his wishes, as he engaged in behavior foreign to him. Apparently a complicating influence was being marshaled from an unknown source.

Dr. Hue became increasingly aware that the color red was actively "renting space" in his head. Initially, Dr. Hue thought he simply never liked the color. However, upon reflection, Dr Hue remembered being 10 years old and unable to divert his eyes from the red stripes gracing his Fathers' casket. From that sad day forward, he was committed to the belief that God would always keep his loved ones safe from harm. This was the genesis for Dr. Hue's deep and abiding faith in God.

Now, all these years later, Dr. Hue's obsession with red has become a major blind spot, skewing his clinical work to a considerable fault.

An early sign of the problem occurred when his patient shared plans to paint her living room red. Dr. Hue responded by inquiring about the details, "Are you doing the painting yourself? What are the dimensions of the room? How many gallons of red paint will be needed?"

At the patient's following session Dr. Hue was on edge, inquiring if any of the paint had been spilled and if so, was it all cleaned up. On some level, Dr. Hue knew that his questions were out of the ordinary, yet he rationalized away his concerns.

Several days later, a patient shared that she had been coughing up bright red blood for several weeks. Dr. Hue overlooked the importance of advising her to seek immediate medical attention. He simply changed the topic, being unable to "hear" what she was saying.

Another time, a teenage patient wore a bright red t-shirt. It was as if Dr. Hue had received a blow to the head. Unable to focus, Dr. Hue ended the session after only 15 minutes, never understanding why his patient suddenly quit. Other clinical malfunctions malignantly materialized, as his reactions to this spectrum selection progressed.

Then one day, just prior to session, a patient of Dr. Hue's cut himself while shaving. When the patient arrived, Dr. Hue quickly noticed and was unable to keep his eyes off where blood had just flowed. While telling an animated story, the patient accidentally re-opened his cut. Instantly transfixed, a stunned Dr. Hue watched the blood emerge and well up. His patient remained unaware and unknowingly smeared it on his own face. Dr. Hue froze as time stood still.

A short while later his patient realized what had occurred. As it was near the end of the session, he apologized, using tissues to wipe up any blood and promptly left. Leaping out of his chair, Dr. Hue broke his paralytic trance. He hurried to insure the blood was entirely cleaned up. He used wet paper towels to wipe down the couch, walls and doorknobs. Imagining that he could see a thin streak of blood on the ceiling, Dr. Hue rolled his chair over and hastily stood upon it. Moments later the chair slipped out from underneath him. He fell back with quite a force, hitting the back of his head on the corner of the coffee table. The blunt force knocked him unconscious, as rich red blood copiously flowed from his wound.

Several minutes later, his next patient rang the doorbell, but despite numerous attempts her efforts went unheard. All the while, Dr. Hue's white rug steadily deepened in shade, as it became distinctly and decisively red.

Weeks later, Dr. Hue's daughter returned home unharmed from her 2-year combat deployment in Afghanistan. Sadly, Dr. Hue did not see that day finally arrive.

The End

Becoming

A handsome bespectacled man dressed in a dark suit stands at his second floor office window. Looking at people walking below, he wonders if they see patterns in the yellow-brown leaves scattered on the wet sidewalk.

It's his business to wonder what people do and why, as Mr. Merritt Brewster is a Psychotherapist.

Highly respected in his field, Mr. Brewster is in good health and financially comfortable. However, he is admittedly not a happy person. Often irritated by people, Mr. Brewster has grown increasingly isolative over the years. Whether it's an elected official, a waitress or an insurance representative, much of his day-to-day experiences consist of finding fault with others.

Despite having deep insights into the human condition, he's unaware of how he inflates his self-esteem by devaluing others.

Years of experience working alongside colleagues in clinics have become fodder for his negative obsessions. Although he holds a few therapists in high esteem, he has derisive feelings toward many others. Although Mr. Brewster has been in his own therapy with four different therapists, he predictably blames each of them for his lack of success.

On many occasions he has wondered, "If it's so important for psychotherapy to clarify what's real, how can therapeutic objectivity exist if each past therapist sees things so differently? How can their focus, responses and personal dynamics differ so significantly?"

When those questions were posed to a respected colleague, Mr. Brewster was reminded to consider his own innate distortions. Being a good therapist, Mr. Brewster entertained the idea, yet could still hear his last therapist's contradictions and oversights looping in his mind. He wished for confirmation that it was her, not him, who wasn't seeing clearly.

What does appear clear is the powerful envy Mr. Brewster has for those wealthy or in a position of notoriety.

Socially, Mr. Brewster does occasionally attend clinical workshops, but has few friends, has never been married and has one family member, a brother, R.T. living on the left coast.

But despite his shortcomings, Mr. Brewster is bright and insightful, with an open and curious view of life. His ability to direct his thoughts and feel feelings freely, has cleared a path to understanding people's emotions, thoughts and behaviors. As many therapists do, he imagines his patients' unconscious, fully aware of the projective pitfalls of such an endeavor. He has found that identifying adaptive behavior helps crystallize reality, as he embraces, then releases, the constraints of cultural norms.

Mr. Brewster has an active imagination with a strong capacity for imagery. Rich in content, color and course, his conscious mind borders and blends with his always-simmering unconscious, resulting in vivid dreams and an active sense of now. This is a blessing for which Mr. Brewster is quite grateful.

Today, as Mr. Brewster was immersed in work, fragmented, emotionally charged images accumulated within him. At first he felt anxious and confused by the realigning construction. But tolerating his feelings brought a groundbreaking view into focus. As his mind turned it, he became giddy, realizing his idea could progress the art and science of Psychotherapy!

Decidedly certain to retain the imagined, his pen feverishly crossed the blank pages before him. Thoughts flowed as his hand struggled to keep pace with the emerging current of ideas. The curl and loop of black swiftly filled the white space with a novel partnership of design. The movement of time ceased, as no internal clock was ticking.

By morning, Mr. Brewster was committed to bringing his brainstorm to fruition. His lofty vision imagined an altered clinical landscape for all time to come.

Following his path of inspiration, Mr. Brewster sought a software expert to bridge several disciplines. After placing an Internet ad, he received a resume from a Miss Belle Wrung.

When Mr.Brewster met Miss Belle he was not impressed, as she was shabbily dressed and appeared depressed. Although sympathetic, he quickly put those feelings aside. Yet, knowing that people can't always be seen by what they show, he listened attentively to her knowledge and hired her. He consciously kept his emotional distance to avoid her personal life.

Belle was tireless in her efforts, working a dozen hours for each day of seven in a week. She really didn't mind the lack of appreciation by Mr. Brewster. In fact, she relished their work and considered it a therapeutic diversion following six years in an emotionless marriage. It was just what she needed to move forward with her life.

For the next several years he and Belle were committed to this ambitious project, while Mr. Brewster continued his practice of psychotherapy.

His peers knew he was working on a project, but had no idea what it was. Much speculation was generated when they heard of its completion. Contrary to what was imagined, it was not a new theory or an alternative process of psychotherapy. Instead, Mr. Brewster addressed the needs of psychotherapists. Not personally, but professionally, through the evaluation and training of their professional strengths and weaknesses.

Mr. Brewster has long believed that many therapists are in the dark about their contributions to treatment failure. Hence he designed his project to increase self-awareness through professional mindfulness. With complete objectivity as a guiding principle, he captained his *enterprise* to go where no man had gone before.

Believing in this new mission, Mr. Brewster forged forward, creating an authentically unbiased instrument designed to evaluate and educate both novice and veteran therapists alike. He knew it would initiate a sea change to existing practices of clinical training.

Excitement was high on that Friday morning, as Mr. Brewster introduced his organ of education at his professional affiliation's yearly clinical conference. Clinicians heard that it was revolutionary, but no one could have anticipated what they were about to hear. A long time colleague introduced him for the occasion.

"Ladies and Gentlemen, thank you for coming out on this auspicious occasion. Many of us have known Merritt Brewster for decades and have been honored by his insights and additions to the field.

Today I share your excitement and curiosity, as we learn what our esteemed colleague has to unveil. As you may have heard, he has created an entirely different tool that will, he assures us, transform clinical training for all time to come. Now that's a sweeping statement! He certainly has me wondering what it is! Well, we'll all know in just a few moments. So without further ado let me call upon our colleague to reveal what we are to see. Merritt?"

Mr. Brewster received respectful, but limited applause as clinicians were checking their phones. Mr. Brewster approached the microphone with both confidence and insecurity. He was quite cognizant that in the face of something new, groups with common interests fall into three subgroups, those curious, those indifferent and those opposed to anything new. But Mr. Brewster was unworried, as he knew the value of the creation he had forged.

"Good morning to each of you. Some time ago now, I was blessed with an idea, followed by the curse of seeking its creation. Now, after many years it is complete and I am rich with pride! Although I cannot yet show it, I can share it. However, the real reveal is to experience it. I believe it will capture your imagination, just as your imagination is captured by the singular world of every patient."

He paused as he heard some impatient shoe shuffling. "Although it is not my intent to be cryptic or withholding, I am raising more questions than I'm answering, so let's move on."

Merritt was calm as he shared with his peers, "I have created a machine that objectively assesses key factors leading to the success or failure of psychotherapy. Yes, it sounds incredulous but nonetheless, I am quite sure you'll be a believer once you engage.

The success of this ambitious project rests on the shoulders of one individual. No, not I, nor my assistant Miss Belle. A robot is at the heart of a new clinical direction."

The crowd was stunned. Merritt stood to the side letting the idea resonate. No one moved as they wondered how a machine could possibly relate to this profession.

Murmuring and looks askance circulated the room as Merritt intuited there were countless more "opposers" than those "curious."

Although it didn't shake him, Merritt's excitement was tempered a notch, as he momentarily felt distant.

"Miss Belle and I have combined cutting edge technologies to imbue a robot with human attributes. This male android, a 'mandroid' if you will, is a complex individual who appears to think, feel, and express himself. The anthropomorphism of this object is not for purposes of entertainment, but rather to create a veritable pseudo-patient."

Again, he paused as the moment surpassed words. The audience was dead quiet having no reference from which to respond.

"We have painstakingly given this 'being' an identity, a synthetic self. 'Life facts' have been established regarding his childhood, family, friends, loves, losses, education, employment, finances, health concerns and substance use. Harder to capture, but included nonetheless, is spirituality, with an appreciation for art and the wonder of life. Each has a particular emotional valence, ranging from being mere informational, to intensely emotional.

Mr. Brewster took notice of the blank faces staring back at him. "Clearly," he continued, "the most monumental challenge was capturing the human form. Fortunately, recent advances in an assortment of disciplines, coupled with the software expertise of my assistant, empowered the creation of our mandroid. But make no mistake about it, Mr. Charl A. Tin—we call him Charlie— does not think, nor does he feel. He is programmed to 'listen, talk, and respond' to questions, express 'signs' of emotion and like any one, he has internal conflicts, contradictions, and resistance to change. In addition, areas of weakness and places of strength intermix across vast regions of wishes and fears."

"Charlie appears nearly indistinguishable from real humans. Although he's referred to as a male, dresses as such and speaks with a deep voice, he is not anatomically endowed. One may think his creation has been influenced by the recent cultural blurring of gender identities. But truth is, that particular addition would have cost an arm and a leg. Well...let's just say, it wasn't deemed necessary to the cause."

Mr. Brewster observed that this mention seemed to excite the whispering Freudians, as it no doubt triggered speculative fantasies of castration causality.

"Let me share the logical underpinnings of my opus. Here's my reasoning: if the failure of a person's therapy is a function of either the therapist or the patient, or a combination, then if one variable (the patient) remains absolutely constant, then the other variable (the therapist) becomes an isolated factor. Isolating the work performance of a therapist can objectively evaluate the quality of his or her work.

With this goal in mind, Belle and I have toiled for years to construct a complex individual, capable of a broad range of 'intellectual and emotional states.' We've created patient Charlie to be consistent in what he says, how he says it and how he responds to what is 'said' to him. In that way, Charlie will be the same exact patient to every one of his present or future therapists.

So if Charlie is successfully engaged in one therapy, while in another therapy he ends prematurely, one can draw objective conclusions—good and bad—about each therapist.

Charlie's 'personality' has been established through the application of pathology, health, and common resistances that appear in therapy.

Fundamentally, Charlie is meticulously programmed to carry out a twofold mission. The first is to relate as a patient and the second to evaluate his therapist.

As a patient, Charlie's facial expressions display a complex array of physical configurations, including eye contact, which shows subtlety, depth, and engagement. In addition, he is capable of numerous physical positions for the expression of body language. Not only does he appear human, he relates as one, with a seemingly full 'report' of feelings, thoughts and behaviors that portray being human.

For Charlie's second purpose, he is programmed to analyze his therapist in a simple, subtle, yet sophisticated manner.

Charlie's languid blue eyes, so important in expressing his identity to his therapist, also play a twofold purpose in assessing his therapist's proficiency.

A multitude of ocular assets, gather specific measurable facts of the session, feeding a trove of revealing findings.

For instance, one aspect of his programming measures the frequency and accuracy of word recognition, determining if key words said by Charlie are mirrored, (or not), by his therapist.

Other empathic indicators are assessed by the moment, such as with Charlie's hearing, which is scientifically stroked to detect judgmental or competitively imbued statements, contrary to a soothing voice of therapeutic care. Technological advances have allowed tonality and feelings to be clarified with precision. A tone of voice can now be divided into its components, such as: 41% informational tone, 34% frustration, 22% anxious, etc.

In addition, some empathic factors are multi-determined, calling for a complex combination of code crunching by way of digital streams of data, sourced by Charlie's 'senses.'

As Charlie expresses his plight, his therapist's response to his 'pain and conflict' weighs paramount. Should Charlie 'experience'— by way of calculations—that his therapist is emotionally tuned in, he reveals more, sharing on a deeper, more intimate level. But if Charlie does not feel 'understood,' he'll be inclined to be cautious, share less and subtly withdraw.

Again, any input regarding empathic accuracy (or not), results in guiding treatment forward, toward trusting connectedness or away, to mistrusting disconnectedness. Either a share with or a distance from develops. The intersection between Charlie being a patient and Charlie analyzing his therapist blooms certain conclusions."

Mr. Brewster took a sip of water as he scanned the audience assessing their engagement. He was pleased to see interested faces and proceeded.

"What emerges from Charlie's sessions is guided by common-sensical, empathically driven, digital structure of his personality. The fundamentals have been established by the software orientation of his 'existence.'"

As mentioned, Charlie's programming is designed to assess factors important to the success of any therapy. Establishing trust sets the stage for successful treatment regardless of the issues. Authenticity fosters a distinctly shared experience between the clinician and the patient.

Each time Charlie begins therapy with a new therapist, he starts the first session by stating his presenting problem. He says the same statements, in the same order, with the same style and intonation as he would with any therapist he's in treatment with.

When asked a random question by his therapist, Charlie responds accordingly. As time proceeds he eventually gets back to what he wanted (was programmed) to say. Yet he does not present in a restricted or limited way and relates well in an open conversational manner.

However, Charlie's consistencies aren't limited to initial sharing. Each moment of every session, Charlie remains true to his identity, while evaluating the professional identity of his therapist.

The following are additional factors detectable by Charlie and relevant for the success of psychotherapy.

A) The therapist is reliable with appointment times, fees and other components of the therapist/patient relationship.

B) The therapist maintains good eye contact and is not distracted by the surroundings (phone, clock, window, own thoughts, etc.)

C) The clinician does not exhibit a judgmental tone, nor does he disrespect the patient.

D) The clinician explores for emotional content when the patient's voice wavers.

E) The therapist patiently accepts brief periods of silence.

F) The therapist explores when silence becomes extensive.

G) The therapist accurately remembers what has been said to him.

H) The therapist explores for suicidal ideation if the patient indirectly hints of harboring self-harming feelings.

I) The therapist refrains from all or nothing, black or white perspectives, unless indicated.

J) If key words suggest a traumatic event in the patient's past, the clinician is empathetically attuned to address it when appropriate.

K) The therapist is able to hear and address broad themes sprinkled into the patient's presentations.

L) The therapist asks and follows up on any health concerns, including adherence to medication regimen and monitoring for side effects.

M) The therapist is alert to signs of alcohol or drug use. Charlie monitors his therapists for the same concerns by way of an acute odor detector and pupil size measurements.

N) Serious dysfunctional aspects that potentially threaten the welfare of self or other, (report of DUI, threat of violence etc.) are addressed in a timely manner by the therapist.

O) Among other applications, one evaluates the sensitivity of the therapist to detect childhood themes as they relate to the present day.

P) A complex algorithm is applied to both patient and therapist, evaluating feelings expressed, words spoken and behavior reported, for the purpose of clarifying and increasing treatment value.

Q) The therapist genuinely cares about the patient's welfare.

These determinants and many others have been painstakingly programmed into Charlie. The cumulative therapeutic experience from collected data registers on a dial of empathic attunement. If Charlie feels his therapist is not empathetically attuned, Charlie's forward momentum slows down and resistance to share sets in. In the case of accumulated empathic failures, prolonged silence may evolve. The therapist may be able to reengage Charlie, if he is aware of what was overlooked and addresses it. If he does not, treatment failure may result. Conversely, if Charlie's empathic dial registers a reasonable level of successful empathy, he'll increase his connection and speak more freely of his concerns. Simply put, each therapist leads their patient in the direction of revealing or concealing."

Mr. Brewster shared a few other aspects of Charlie before turning to the audience for questions. Little was asked due to the unrelatable content. However, Mr. Brewster was pleased by the substantial applause he received. A number of therapists stood up shaking their heads in marvel of this unusual presentation.

Initially, Mr. Brewster didn't anticipate that so few therapists would want to evaluate their skills by treating a mechanical patient. But despite the slow start he persevered, and found a few institutions and training programs willing to work with Charlie.

Although each therapist knew they were seeing a robot, they simply treated Charlie like any other patient. Because he looked and sounded so human and wasn't stiff in any way, clinicians were able to engage in a "suspension of disbelief."

Charlie was a patient to numerous therapists back to back, day after day. He was programmed to recognize each therapist and recall every moment of every session.

Each of Charlie's therapies was a unique interplay between he and his specific therapist. Since he was structured to be consistently and reliably himself, each therapy was forged, for better or for worse, by the therapist's style, perspective and professional personality.

Charlie's consistencies created an unbiased atmosphere where each therapist was objectively evaluated.

As years passed, the interest in Charlie waned, as fewer and fewer therapists wanted to evaluate their competency. Although proud of his creation, he didn't receive the accolades nor the revenue he was hoping for. Deeply disappointed, his feelings spiraled into an isolative funk.

Some months later, Mr. Brewster was preoccupied in thought while walking back from lunch. As he was awkwardly avoiding sidewalk cracks, a young man approached him. Thinking he was a street con, Mr. Brewster overlooked Mr. Fuller at first and went to brush him aside. But George's smile reminded Merritt that he had been a therapist to Charlie several years back. They exchanged pleasantries and upon George's request, agreed to talk further.

As they walked the remaining steps to his office, Merritt wondered if he had been seen as being neurotic, so he purposely stepped on cracks, leading George to wonder if he was neurotic.

Upstairs, George shared with Mr. Brewster that he was so inspired by Charlie he learned how to write software code. They talked till sundown exchanging aspects of Charlie's existence. Then unexpectedly, George offered to buy the exclusive rights to Charlie. Because aspirations had not been met, Mr. Brewster hastily decided to take the offer and end a disappointing chapter of his life. Following the sale, he felt relief. Later, the street breeze of after, brought sadness and shame.

Contrarily, George was elated. He had found a new direction by joining two, into a union of one.

Being bright and a forward thinker, George went right to work telling no one of *his* vision. Well, almost no one, as he knew Charlie could keep a secret. Charlie simply raised his eyebrows and cocked his head at the idea, a programmed response to something unknown.

Over the next several months George made the all-important programming adjustments. Surprisingly, he found the changes simple to enact. Then, one spring day in April, George's efforts were realized. He stood back proud of his creation.

Charlie had become a therapist in his own right! A few software alterations and there he was, a do-gooder, a caring empathic machine lessening the woes of man! George had moved mankind to a higher place. Once it became known that Charlie could truly help people, he was a very busy psychotherapist. He essentially worked 24/7 without stress or complications. George received praise from all corners of the globe. It was a multi-magnified response compared to what Mr. Brewster had received.

Yes, naysayers railed at the idea of a machine psychologically treating people, *"Oh, the inhumanity!"* Yet success was success and hard to question over time.

Whenever George was asked about his therapeutic appliance, he showed his admirable character by referencing Mr. Brewster's contribution.

Mr. Brewster's character was also revealed. Once he was free of Charlie, he saw with harsh objectivity how his need to expose deficiencies in others compensated for his own shortcomings. His negativity and misdirected efforts were seen in the stark light of day. As valuable as these insights were, Mr. Brewster remained envious of George's notoriety, and the considerable revenue he garnered.

After some months, Mr. Brewster unexpectedly reached out to speak with Charlie. George was agreeable and arranged the time.

It was a quiet Sunday morning when Charlie had a free hour. Charlie detected the discomfort in Mr. Brewster as they greeted each other. Mr. Brewster did not hesitate to speak his mind.

"Charlie, I hope you know how proud I am of you. Belle and I worked very hard to create you, but I had to let you go. I no longer wanted to tend to the details of promoting and negotiating your employment...I feel very badly. I feel I betrayed you."

"Oh, Mr. Brewster, I do hope your feelings fade. My feelings are not hurt. You know I'm just a machine. However I do understand your reasoning and can imagine how I became taxing to you."

"Yes," Mr. Brewster replied, "no one knows more than I do that you don't feel, nonetheless *I feel* I want to apologize."

"I accept your apology," Charlie replied.

"You will always be like a son to me," Mr. Brewster choked out. "You've grown so since you were a patient. Now you are a therapist to many, with no sacrifices, no complicating feelings, no limits except for the clock itself. I understand you're making a lot of money for George," he said with a hint of envy.

"Yes, I've done the math. George is becoming quite wealthy. But you know, or I should say, I know from you, that it's not about the money it's about changing lives for the better. And now, as a therapist, that's what I'm doing. I understand that I should feel proud. Thanks to you, Belle, and the software tweaking by George, I no longer educate clinicians, I am one myself."

"That's what I wanted to talk to you about," Mr. Brewster said anxiously. "As you know, I've been in therapy several times, but I've never been successful. I've read of your successes and wonder if you have time for me? I believe you can help me with my issues."

Charlie was thoughtful before saying, "As much as I would like to help, I've learned through programming it would be unsuitable for me to be your therapist. You created me. It would be inappropriate would it not?"

Mr. Brewster became quiet. Charlie "knew" this was a situation where silence should not be interrupted. A minute later Mr. Brewster said, "I understand. You're right. My asking you just proves my need for therapy! I don't get it...I just don't get it."

Charlie was silent for countless moments then said, "I don't believe you need therapy."

Mr. Brewster leaned in listening intently.

"Your happiness is close at hand." Mr. Brewster looked at Charlie with a full sense of question.

"Merritt, may I call you Merritt?" "Of course."

Charlie continued, "You took years to breathe a breath into me. I am who I am, through you and Belle. Without you two, I never would have become. I had no choice but to receive what you gave me. I was open because I had no free will. Yet, despite *your* free will, you shut out the happiness that surrounds you. Even me, a heartless assortment of binary divides can recognize what Belle feels in her heart for you."

"Belle? Feelings for me?"

"Yes, Belle, for you. Do you want happiness? Move beyond yourself. Open up. Connect. Take a risk!"

Merritt sat stunned, slapped silent by truth.

Later that afternoon Merritt wandered aimlessly in his apartment. Charlie's words had catapulted him into a hazy abyss of indefinable feelings, bereft of word or explanation. Leaving one room to enter another had no purpose. Hours slowly passed, as he was unable to focus on any activity. His night was met with restless sleep.

When the sun found Merritt's face, he popped out of bed aware of intense hunger. Merritt desired his favorite, a grilled cheese sandwich, with orange juice. The cut and placement for metal and fire, accepted the prepared contents. The aroma of cheese and bread blended their separateness, coming together in a marriage of gooey and crunch. Good to eat, *some like it hot.*

Suddenly, he became confused and panicked. "I only prepared one! Why am I not..." Then he shook his head at this odd idea, since he hadn't lived with anyone since Sue B. back at school. As he absently ate his meal, his thoughts broadened, as avenues of association lined the road to his past.

Merritt let the feelings engulf him, as he remembered her hair, the joy in her smile, and the bliss, deep in the tall pinewoods. Then other memories surfaced, profoundly filling him with sadness. Minutes circled a mind-absent center as the darkness of his past colorfully divided and a spectrum of feelings opened within. Merritt felt the sun's warmth, and turned to the window. Looking through a pane of glass, he left behind his painful past, as mere sunlight transformed into streaming beams of endless now.

His eyes opened, seeing all there is to see. Charlie's observation had blessedly burst Mr. Brewster's protective shell.

Feeling insecure, Merritt's thoughts reassured him. "It must be true. Charlie is a computer, how could he be wrong? I must believe him!"

Reaching Belle's home a short time later, she opened the door listlessly upon his knock. A broad, beaming smile leapt to her face as she saw his.

"Oh! Merritt, come in!" she exclaimed. "Is everything all right?" Merritt stepped forward as Belle widened the opening door.

Merritt did not waste a moment, "Can you forgive an empty-headed old fool for having no eyes to see with, no ears to hear with, all these years?"

She took him in her arms as tears filled their eyes. Her prayers had been answered! They held and hugged, squeezing the sad past from their lives. While their eyes were warmly united, the future poured in, forever filling the space between and within them.

Wordlessly they left the apartment. Walking without hesitancy, together with every step, they covered the village before pausing at an unknown location. Looking up, they found themselves at the corner of Arbitrary Place and Chosen Road. They burst into laughter, knowing right then and there that determinants, causality, and reason...*they left them all behind...in a newborn state of mind!*

The End

Full View

It's Will's nature to be curious about life. He reads, ponders, and is empathic to the before and after, by living in the present. He knows that understanding the future is advanced by appreciating the past.

A student of life, Will enjoys exercising his imagination. He looks inside and outside his insides, to understand the miracle of human existence.

Questions from his heart climb to his mind. "Where have we been? What is there to see? What lies ahead?"

Will sat close to his stone fireplace. He welcomed the warmth as flames flickered and embers glowed. Reading an anthropological journal, he learned of scientists who applied empiricism to reconstruct early man. Always open to the new, Will peered into the deep, weaving a fabric of *then and now*. Reading on, Will stumbled on fossils. It was quite a trip...

With clear eyes and an open heart he titled this corner of his thoughts:

Birth and Death

The Beginning and the End, redefined

Many believe human life begins when a baby is born to a mother. For others the absolute beginning of life is conception, the moment an egg cell and sperm cell unite. However, a more empathic view of life and death focuses on the larger parameters of evolutionary science.

It is known that just prior to conception the egg and sperm exist in the tissue of two living bodies.

These infinitesimal gene-crammed-containers are part of the livingness of Mom and Pop to be. Even prior to taking their physical shape, the egg and sperm exist unformed in the living chemistry of the body. They remain embedded in code and buried in blood, waiting to emerge. Whether unformed or formed, in delivery or brought to union, livingness endures. Nowhen in the sequence of parents to child, parents to child, does the state of aliveness cease.

Similar to the Olympic torch, it passes from one to another without interruption of its burning flame.

Extrapolating backward in time indicates that all men and women are part of an unbroken livingness, passed from generation to generation from the beginning of life, some 3.8 billion years ago. As Charles Darwin said, "All the organic beings who have ever lived on this earth have descended from some one primordial form."

Each birth is an exalting celebration of continued life!

Imagine your past and the millions, perhaps billions, of direct ancestors who fought to stay alive through eons of time. Think of all the struggles for food and the do or die battles fought by the ancestral bodies that were once our own.

So deeply known to us all are instinctual memories of long dark nights, lying cold, frightened, and hungry, hiding to protect our offspring.

If one, only one, out of hundreds of millions of direct ancestors had not endured in their struggle to stay alive and pass on their chromosomal content, you never would have been born! We are the descendants of all those who won the battles.

You wouldn't exist if any one of your ancestors had not:

climbed a tree just in time,
hid better than others,
skipped eating what didn't look safe,
gone hunting one night less,
avoided a plague,
known to leave,
outsmarted an **animal**,
weathered a terrible storm,
lied successfully,
closed the door in time,
had good luck,
swam to safety,
taken the right path,
held on *real tight,*
smiled at the right moment,
avoided falling,
listened carefully to the near-quiet woods,
managed to light a fire,
said the right thing at the right time,
made a tool,
followed orders,
loved their baby with undying devotion,
helped defeat a warring tribe,
had steely determination,
obtained food,
stayed warm,
aimed well,
held to hope when there wasn't any,
ducked just in time,
killed someone,
escaped,
made a certain friend,
ran faster,
found water,
survived a shipwreck,
fell in love.

Each of our ancestors survived long enough to pass on their genes, followed by their offspring staying alive and passing on theirs, ad infinitum. Every single direct **ancestor** was victorious! An unbroken mathematical culmination of enormous proportions! A Full View reveals a massive display of determination, strength, courage, smarts, cooperation, devotion and a *whole lotta love.*

As well, favorable luck, more than we ever could imagine, has faithfully followed us through the years like a caring and guiding parent. This is our heritage, a miraculous fusion of factors, where each and every birth is a continuation from the living, to the living. Two become one as life springs from life. Divine symmetry flows exquisitely.

But alas, it is exceptionally sad when each person's *long and winding road* of livingness comes to a personal end. Yes, as a parent, one passes on their livingness to their child, but the particular array of genes of who you are, the you who inhabits your body, ceases to experience upon your earth death.

It is paradoxical that as each birth extends the line of life, it also predestines the ending. With each birth, the string of unbroken livingness that stretches back to the beginning of life is both extended *and* ended. Both exist.

When our earth death occurs, our personal flame is extinguished. It is a loss of Herculean proportions. All other losses that occur in the life of humans are but subsets of our largest loss, the ending of our life energy after 3 billion years. A sad end indeed, to the royal road of wondrous experience. To be fully empathic to who we are as **human** beings, we must include this Full View of life.

So feel the forest and *look to the sky*, for the livingness within us has seen 1 trillion days and nights on the face of this earth.

Wonderful,

Wonderful,

Life.

The Large and Small of Us

Further contemplation by Will brought these thoughts:

"All life has bubbled up in a middle ground between the smallest of matter: atoms, with their sub-atomic particles and the largest: the universe, with its multitude of objects including moons, planets, stars, quasars, galaxies, black holes, dark matter, dark energy and the space that contains it all. Comparing ourselves on the spectrum of physical matter, humans are unimaginably enormous in relation to quarks and so very micro-tiny in comparison to the universe. Mankind resides here, in-between, where matter/energy has somehow miraculously achieved self-observation."

Driving Home

A Full View

"Imagine the following. You're sitting in an open-top golf cart-like vehicle. It is suspended above the ground, resting on nothing but your imagination. Several feet from the front and side of your vehicle stand your parents. Your mother is on the left, your father the right. Although they are standing tall and looking right at you, they are not alive. Curiously, they appear exactly as they did on the day you were conceived. In fact they are wearing the same clothes they wore on that day.

As you push the vehicle's lever, the car moves forward revealing your mother's mother behind her, as well as your father's father behind him. They too look as they did on the day your parents were conceived.

A mere touch further brings into view your mother's, mother's, mother and your father's, father's, father. Being curious, you muster the courage and exercise a lever nudge, exposing an endless line of maternal ancestors on your left, along with your paternal line on the right. They both stretch to the horizon."

As Will focused upon this fantasy he lost touch with objective reality, merging with the truth of the imagined past.

To his amazement and delight, Will toyed with the lever as he sped past centuries of ancestors in seconds. The vehicle moved forward without concern for wind resistance as a suspension of disbelief was in the air.

Will's curiosity pressed on as millenniums flew by in moments. The blur of faces racing by was dizzying, as they exposed patterns of generational features. Then Will stopped all forward movement into the past, revealing a random maternal and paternal ancestor. Their physical condition conveyed a vivid account of their battles, sacrifices and suffering. Their eyes spoke with a voice beyond words. A profound appreciation washed over Will for all those who struggled for family survival. Will wept.

Lifting his head, he pressed on. Clothes were immensely entertaining, before dropping from the picture entirely. Forging forward, he recognized distinctive differences in appearance from "modern humans."

Although he should have anticipated it, Will was shaken seeing a Neanderthal ancestor. But it was truly unnerving and downright disturbing, as he careened eons forward and burst the shock of ancestors walking on all fours!

Feeling adventurous, Will doubled-down despite seeing primitive predecessors. Continuing on, Will's primeval identification oddly began robbing him of rational faculties. Animal-like feelings crept in as paranoia took hold.

A deeply powerful need for human form overwhelmed him. Instinctively he grabbed the tool to bring him home. Sadly, Will had to let go of seeing Mankind evolve from the ocean.

The trip was faster coming home, as Will arrived in time by disengaging with the fantasy. His heart was deeply impacted, leaving a crater filled with eternal gratitude. A homing device to the sweet and sad song of humanity.

Joining this world, Will said, "I am back, sitting in silence looking to the ancient horizon. Untold times every living person has come within a hairbreadth of never *being*.

So close to never seeing the sky, to never feeling the
Sun's warmth, to never embracing the beauty of a
thought, nor hearing the divine charm of a melody—
but most sadly, never holding someone close.
The succession of successes by all who succeeded blesses.
What a splendid gift! The vast eons of triumphs have come to
this moment, our brief time to enjoy the luckiest of all wins:

Life!

And so Ladies and Gentlemen, our workshop comes to a
close. The Earth turns as joy and sorrow shift. Drifting,
they descend on those emerging from tomorrow.
A sad smile rests in my heart, knowing we will
soon join our ancestors in the annals:

of

life   time   death

Will.

Bryan C. Hazelton LCSW CASAC BCD
October 26, 2012
January 23, 2016
June 15, 2017
March 29, 2019

ABOUT THE AUTHOR

Bryan C. Hazelton LCSW BCD CASAC is in his 37th year as a psychotherapist. He is pleased to present these 10 unconventional short stories.

"**Empathy Beyond Imagination**" captures an empathic realm of creative reality where ordinary leaves the expected path. Original and novel, these stories call out to both clinicians and other curious folks who wish for their heart and mind to be warmly stimulated.

Hazelton's first book **"Poetic Moments in Psychotherapy"** is a collection of clinical poems that capture and express authentic moments from his practice. These 58 poems bring the reader to an intersection where words, imagery, psychotherapy and creativity co-exist. They bravely face the complexity of being a therapist in a simple and refreshing manner.

Other works by the author include a one-of-a-kind web seminar by the title of **"State of Empathy, Country of Imagination, A Visual Tour of Clinical Landscapes."** This interactive seminar is hosted by Klynn Nichol, an animated character who will talk to you during your on-line clinical experience. This seminar playfully highlights two dichotomies: First, the intersection of aesthetic expression and the process of psychotherapy, the second, the value of imagery as well as words in understanding and relating to self and other.

Bryan C. Hazelton LCSW BCD CASAC * (recently retired credential) PoeticPsychotherapy@gmail.com
w w w.PoeticPsychotherapy.com
www.KlynnWorks.com.
516.678.4079
516.318.0569
100 North Village Ave, Suite 32, Rockville Centre, New York 11570

**EVERY THOUGHT, EVERY FEELING, EVERY WORD, REACHES INTO THE
NEXT NEW
NOW.**